I0763499

# Trolldom

*Unlocking the Traditional Magic Practice of Sweden, Norway, Denmark, and Finland*

## Your Free Gift
## (only available for a limited time)

Thanks for getting this book! If you want to learn more about various spirituality topics, then join Mari Silva's community and get a free guided meditation MP3 for awakening your third eye. This guided meditation mp3 is designed to open and strengthen ones third eye so you can experience a higher state of consciousness. Simply visit the link below the image to get started.

**https://spiritualityspot.com/meditation**

# Table of Contents

# Introduction

The frozen north doesn't sound like the most magical place on Earth, but this is where we need to go to discover the magic of trolldom and Norse mythology. It has always been an unforgiving place with a harsh climate and hardy people, but maybe these facts make the Nordic ways so compelling. They had to survive their environment and thrive, so the stories that accompanied their history became increasingly enchanting and filled with heroes, heroines, gods and goddesses, and a series of magical beings they needed to defeat to become victorious.

These stories are inspiring and exciting. Bloodthirsty and violent, they also contain all the emotional ups and downs to keep people interested and engaged. The practices of the Nordic folk are what we are going to concentrate on and find a way to connect to these ancient people. The rituals and potions they used have been developed to fit modern times and can be used to make your own form of magic. Why do you need trolldom or any type of magical influence in your life? Maybe you don't need them, but why wouldn't you want them? Broaden your mind and knowledge, and get ready to welcome Nordic ways into your life.

# Chapter 1: Introducing Trolldom

Trolls are generally thought of as cute neon-haired dolls that sit on your desk and are fun to collect. They appear in modern culture, and thanks to the fantasy genre, they have played a part in many movies and books. From the dark, evil creatures featured in J.R.R. Tolkien's sagas to the cute Disney trolls with ribbons in their hair, we have all encountered trolls in one form or another, but what do we really know about them?

They are mythical creatures who have appeared in ancient texts as far back as Norse times, but they probably existed long before. The origin of the name troll has been a cause of disagreement for many experts, and some believe it is derived from the Norse word Jotunn who were giants who inhabited the world before the dawn of humankind. The trolldom we will be considering is a Germanic word that means witchcraft and the practices associated with this particular form of spell work.

We will concentrate on the Scandinavian and Germanic beliefs surrounding trolls and their importance for trolldom. One of the most recognizable tales from Scandinavia featuring the creatures is the story of Three Billy Goats Gruff, in which a fearsome troll guards the bridge the three goats need to cross. The goats are all assorted sizes, sending the smallest goat across the bridge first. The troll threatens to eat the small goat, but it tells the troll if he waits, a larger and more filling meal will come soon. The troll agrees and lets the small goat pass. The second goat then crosses and is stopped by the troll, threatening to eat him. The second goat tells him that a larger goat is coming, which will mean a bigger meal for the troll. The troll agrees and lets him pass. When the third goat attempts to cross the bridge, it calls the troll's bluff and dares him to eat him up. When the troll attacks, the goat knocks him off the bridge with his huge horns, and the troll is swept away by the river. The bridge is now safe for all to pass, and the three goats live happily ever after.

This cautionary tale about greed and being happy with what you have has been a popular children's story since Hans Christian Anderson was introduced to the UK in 1859. A series of Scandinavian and Danish tales have been the staple reading for children ever since.

Some experts believe the troll was part of Prehistoric culture because of cave drawings and other artwork from that age, and the memory of them from Cro-Magnon times has filtered down to Northern Europe as man began to migrate the world. This theory doesn't work for experts who believe trolls originated in Scandinavia because, during that era, a large glacier covered the area that is today known as Scandinavia.

These theories show trolls as part of the forefather cult belief prevalent in the tenth and eleventh centuries - when Scandinavians believed in the power of the dead and ancestors were encouraged to return to the living world and share their powers. The believers would sit on mounds to communicate with the deceased and make contact. When Christianity became popular in Europe, laws were passed to make the practices illegal, and those beliefs were considered evil and dangerous.

This theory also fits with the Norse culture in which trolls were classed as the spirits of the dead who would often visit the living and help them or return to wreak their revenge on those who had caused them harm during their time on Earth. The trolls of Scandinavia and Norway are scary creatures living in mountains and forests and are huge, even giant-sized, and they work with the natural elements surrounding them. Others are shorter and live in caves or underground lairs. They usually have scraggy and unkempt hair, large noses, and sharp teeth. Some even have multiple heads and tails to make their appearance more intimidating.

## Trolldom

The magic associated with the Scandinavian and Norwegian areas still exists today, and some natives even claim to believe in the existence of real trolls. They tell their children stories of these legendary creatures who will escape their natural dwellings to seek out children who have been badly behaved and eat them! In Iceland, there are a series of thirteen troll sons of the famous Gryla who visit children for thirteen days before Christmas and leave a gift for good children and rotting vegetables for naughty children. They are known as the Yule Boys and have become part of the tourist attractions found in the Nordic area.

The magic of trolldom is based on nature and the power of sunlight especially. Because the area has short periods of sunlight, and the dark is a constant state for most people, the power of solar energy is more significant. It has been compared to Norse magic, the pagan spells and working of Wiccans, and the rituals and spells of Hoodoo. All these practices are based on helping people and improving circumstances, although there are some rituals and spells that can cause harm. Magic is a personal choice, and trolldom lets you take aspects from traditional Nordic practices and intersperse them with elements from African American, English, and Germanic folk magic to create a unique cultural practice.

## Spells Included in Trolldom

Using the term "root work" to describe magic gives you a more detailed insight into what the results should be. Spells and potions, rituals, and conjuring should be used to get to the root of your problems and heal them. What is wrong with your love life, or why has your career ground to a halt? Are you unlucky, or could you use some help in legal matters? Some magic is more general and can be used to alter all-encompassing circumstances, while other magic is used to address more definitive problems.

When the people living in the Nordic regions needed help, there were very few options to consider. They lived in small communities and relied heavily upon the magic practices of their culture. When their crops failed, or their children were taken ill, or disappeared, it seemed logical to turn to mythological creatures to seek reasons why these awful things were happening. Today we know that circumstances happen because of forces we can't control mixed with influences that result from our actions. Or, as some people like to say, "sh#t happens", but imagine if your world was so restricted that you believed that trolls and other mythical creatures influenced what happened in your life. How frightening would that be? It is no wonder that magic and the effect it was perceived to have had such a significant effect on everyday life. Pagan heathenry today means that practitioners adapt to nature and its wonders with more modern practices to reconnect to the world and regain some of the power that seems to have been taken away from us by religion, government, and societal taboos.

## Why Is Nordic Magic So Relevant Today?

Consider how traditional religions and society dictate how we should live. There are strict rules and ideals to live up to and harsh judgments for those who don't adhere. Should we be forced to live with such exacting rules and beliefs? More and more people are bucking the trend and embracing a belief that it's okay to be different. Nonconformity is becoming the norm (oh, the irony!), which includes embracing magic and mythology from the past. Nordic mythology is different; it is filled with flawed characters who had faults and were definitely imperfect. They made mistakes, and they were punished. They had unusual love lives and relationships, and they lived colorful lives filled with drama, romance, love, lust, and war.

The beliefs and practices of the Nordic people weren't just mythical, and we can look to the past for proof that this was how they lived their lives. Relics, artifacts, and physical proof of their civilization have been found and have been adopted by modern practitioners to show allegiance to the Nordic ways. Trolldom is a part of the overall belief system based on magic connected to trolls, elves, and dwarves. These mythical beings played an intrinsic role in the lives of the gods and goddesses of the time and influenced their lives hugely.

This book will show you how to cast spells and make potions that have transcended from history to become part of the magic workings performed today. The knowledge of trolldom gives you a deeper understanding of how ingredients and rituals work to influence the power you have over your and other people's lives. Medieval magic doesn't mean it is less effective than modern work. In fact, it is considered more potent because it has survived so long. Magic is often passed down through generations and is improved, adapted, and expanded.

The problems we face today may seem different from the past, but they aren't! We all want better lives, we all face negative forces, and we all have relationship issues. Use trolldom magic, elven and dwarf magic to use your powers to achieve positive outcomes. As you develop your skills, you'll be blessed with a greater understanding of the power of nature and how to harness it.

Imagine your life filled with quests and adventures. New horizons and destinations await you, and the Norse folk magic will keep you safe and ensure you are successful. Using candle magic, sun, moon magic, herbal, crystal, and magical tools, you'll become adept at Norse folk magic and its benefits. Bring the Nordic culture into your lives and celebrate the magic it holds. Holidays and celebrations will become even more special when you embrace trolldom and Norse ways.

## Symbols and Rituals

**The Valknut symbol.**

*https://commons.wikimedia.org/wiki/File:9crossings-knot-symmetric-triangles-quasi-valknut.svg*

Norse magic uses the power of symbols to strengthen its potency. The easiest way to start your work with trolldom is to incorporate some powerful Norse symbols into your life. Use these examples to decorate your home or personal space and become familiar with Norse magic and its powers.

- **The Valknut** is a prominent and powerful representation of the god Odin. It comprises three triangles forming nine points, all surrounded by a circle. The nine points represent the nine worlds in Norse mythology, while the circle represents the perpetuity of humankind through motherhood and birth.
- **Yggdrasil** is the great tree of the world. It is a giant tree with deep roots representing the universe and how we are all connected. The branches connect the nine realms and deliver life-saving water through their boughs. At the end of the world, or Ragnarök, the gods and their enemies will battle it out until all existence is destroyed. There will be a single man and a woman hiding in the trunk of Yggdrasil who will emerge and repopulate the world.
- **The Helm of Awe** is an eight-sided symbol surrounded by a circle of dragon-like creatures joined by their tails. It was drawn on the foreheads of warriors to protect them in battle. Today it is used in tattoo form to give protection or to signal that the wearer is a believer in Asatru, the Viking and Norse religion.
- **The Triple Horn of Odin** is a symbol formed by three horns interlocked to form a solid form surrounded by a circle of decorative runes or leaves, depending on the designer. The story behind the horns is based on the myth that tells the story of two dwarves named Fjalar and Galar, who were so knowledgeable they could answer any question in the universe. They killed the first being known as Kvasir and mixed his blood with honey - a mixture used to fill three horns, and he blessed one of them with the Mead of Poetry. Odin was desperate to drink the mead and made a pact with the mighty giant Gunnloo to take a sip from each for three days. He tricked her and drank the whole horn, which made him turn into an eagle and escape. The symbol represents wisdom and poetic inspiration.

- **The Mjolnir** is also known as the hammer of Thor and was forged by a dwarf. It wasn't just a tool or weapon. It was also used to consecrate marriages and provide the couple with fertility. It is a symbol of strength and protection and was used by other religions in conjunction with the more traditional cross symbol. It is represented by a decorative hammer-shaped symbol, often with the head facing downward.
- **The Swastika** was a Viking/Norse symbol that the Nazi Party seriously misused in the 1930s. Originally it was used to bring prosperity and order to a person who was experiencing chaos and distress. It is considered one of the most significant good luck charms of Norse beliefs but should only be displayed in places where this knowledge is freely available. Don't forget that the swastika can be considered offensive by some because of its history.
- **The Troll Cross** is a circle with two small horns underneath. It is designed to protect the wearer from the dark practices of elves, trolls, and dwarves.
- The three triangles of Odin are a recurring theme in Nordic symbolism. They have multiple meanings and can be used to represent the following:
- **The Three Roots of Yggdrasil** and the connection to the nine realms.
- **The Three Realms** existed before the earth's creation and man's time on the physical plane. There was a land of fire and land of mist and an indistinct space between the two.
- **The Three Grandchildren of Buri**, the first God of Norse mythology - who was licked out of a block of ice by a mythical cow named Audhumla. His son didn't have much effect on Norse tales, but he produced three sons named Odin, Vili, and Ve. They are attributed to bringing life and senses to humankind and improving their existence on Earth.
- **The Three Goddesses of Fate**. Each one represents the past, the future, and the present.

- Symbols surround us and affect our everyday life. Everybody recognizes the golden archway representing a certain burger joint and what the swish on the side of a good pair of trainers means. Advertisers and big companies are merely trading on ancient knowledge, which means one symbol or sign could be more significant than a hundred words. We gain comfort, strength, and protection from things that represent familiarity, and Norse signs work similarly.

Call it what you like, shamanism, heathenry, Asatru, Wiccan, or pagan; these types of magic and beliefs are experiencing a renaissance for a reason. More people are becoming disillusioned with modern life and are turning to the more traditional methods of dealing with life. Trolls, dwarves, elves, and other mystical beings may seem irrelevant but what they stand for isn't. They represent a link to a world that has become diminished by our electronic equipment. As we all know, technology has become the hub of society and rules our everyday lives. While this is an amazing truth, it can lead to society ignoring and damaging nature due to the development and use of electrical devices to run our lives.

Pagan is an umbrella term that covers nature-based beliefs, and it appeals to people who love the Earth and want to preserve it. It is growing in numbers in Europe and America because it appeals to people. The simple ways and links to the earth honor the world we live in and consider every being as equal. No misogyny, racism, judgment, or punishment is associated with paganism, and they include all forms of worship within their ranks. Imagine if that attitude spread, and we became a world that accepted everybody and every belief. Wouldn't that be amazing?

## Magic in Medieval Times

Before Christianity appeared, magic was part of everyday life, and common folk would consult "witch doctors," "wise men," and other members of the community known as the "cunning folk" who influenced specific areas of their lives. They included the Tempestarii, a form of magi known for their influence over the weather. In periods of drought, they would perform rituals and spells to bring rain, and in times of floods, they would ask the gods for dry weather. The significance of their influence cannot be underestimated. The weather decided if the community would eat or starve as their crops were the staple part of their food chain.

Various spells and ointments would be procured to cure ailments that plagued the community. The locals would seek help for the lifting of curses and bring good luck when needed. These practices were only described as witchcraft with the arrival of Christian dominance in Europe. Pope Innocent III deemed pagan ways as devil-worshipping and evil and created a society that hunted down heretics and punished them. Some groups fled to Germany and the Savoy to escape his campaign to abolish their religion, and this became the home of the Cathars and other pagan groups.

As the growth of Christianity continued, the leading theologians of the era decided to demonize these groups, and they spread stories that Cathars and their followers were conducting devil-worshipping rituals filled with sex and evil deity connections. Further edicts from the Church described a world filled with evil demons and dangerous forces that were dedicated to tempting God-fearing Christians from the path of righteousness with promises of sex and debauched rituals. This began the long association of paganism and sex within the Christian faith.

This was not fun for pagans, and the Church was determined to rid the world of witchcraft and demon worship. They trained secular individuals to use any methods they could to force pagans to confess to their ill doings and witchery. This started a period known as the Inquisition, which resulted in the persecution of people who didn't follow Christian beliefs. It was the time of the "witch trials" and barbaric torture that the new orthodox rulings favored. Magic became a word synonymous with evil, and it has taken centuries for that to change.

Luckily, we are a more tolerant society now, and magic is encouraged and welcomed. We will look back at magical practices and explain how they can be used today to help us live better lives.

# Chapter 2: The Cyprianus Tradition

Magic has been around for generations and has evolved because it has been passed down through the ages. These texts and manuscripts are often referred to as grimoires, but in Swedish magic, there is a more menacing term to cover spells and traditions collected through the ages. The Cyprianus texts don't apply to a standard text but are a general term used to cover the collection of spells and works that are indigenous to the Nordic area.

These manuscripts were sought out by common folk and ministers to learn how to summon magic beings and demons, but most forms of the black book were kept by the "cunning folk," the term used for folk healers and wise people who were often the older members of the community who were responsible for healing and thwarting evil. The books became part of folklore, and the owners could only pass them on to their descendants. They were impossible to get rid of in other ways and were impervious to being burned or destroyed by water.

The author was a bishop and martyr who lived in the early times of Christianity and was a sorcerer before his conversion. He attempted to bewitch a female saint but was overcome with faith when she made the sign of the cross above his head. This freed him from his devilish ties and converted him to Christianity. This description of Cyprianus originated in England in the 17th century and bore little resemblance to the Swedish tales of Cyprianus.

The Swedes believe he was an evil figure who originated from Norway and was a close consort of the Devil. One tale speaks of his deeds being so heinous that the Devil threw him out of hell. Cyprianus then exacted his revenge by writing the Cyprianus texts to share his depraved secrets with anyone who wanted to practice them.

In Denmark, the tale of Cyprianus is completely different. Their folklore tells of a Mexican nun who lived a chaste and pious life before the Devil noticed her good work. He captured the nun and cast her into a dungeon in the mid-14th century, where she was so distressed that she ripped off her habit and undergarments and wrote her magic knowledge on the cloth. These texts were found in the castle after her death.

Whatever name you prefer, the truth is that this is a book that needs to be handled with care. It is filled with spells and powerful incantations to summon the devil and give the user immense magical powers. A cautionary tale from German folklore tells the tale of a Russian soldier who faced a bevy of demons when he began to read his comrade's copy of the Cyprianus texts.

## The Soldiers Tale

While seated by a fire, a Russian soldier inadvertently began to read the text his friend had left lying on the ground. A host of menacing demons immediately appeared and demanded that the soldier set them a task. Luckily the soldier knew that the only way to get rid of the demons was to set them a task they couldn't fulfill, so he told them to fill all the baths in the town with water that is transported using a sieve. After just a minute, the demons returned and told the soldier they had completed the task.

They demanded he set them another, and he told them to go to the Governor of the town and take down his house brick by brick without the knowledge of the inhabitants and then rebuild it in the same design. After just a minute, the demons returned, told him they had finished the deed and demanded another.

The soldier was bemused but thought he had a task they couldn't complete when he told them to visit the Volga River and count every grain of sand, every fish and how many droplets of water the river contained from its source to the mouth. They flew away but quickly returned with the answers he demanded. The soldier was at a loss to think of another task, and the demons were getting restless and threatened him with death if he didn't set them another task soon.

The soldier realized the spirits wouldn't come near him when he had the book in his hands. He picked the book up and began to read it, but the spirits increased and began to press him to act. He thought that if reading the book attracted the spirits, what would happen if he read it backward? He proceeded to read it from the end to the beginning, and he soon noticed that the spirits were fading and leaving the area. As he read on, they disappeared until he was left alone with the book. When his comrade returned, the soldier told him what had happened, and his comrade congratulated him on his actions. He confirmed that if he had continued to read traditionally, the demons would have consumed him on the stroke of midnight.

The spells are a mixed bag of folk remedies, incantations, and prayers with magical connections. They are as simple as healing a sprain or performing divination. Because the text is so diverse, the spells included are a fascinating collection of Nordic magic beliefs and practices.

## To Heal a Sprained Foot

The incantation contains a poem about Jesus and his journey over the rocky ground on his horse. The horse stumbled and twisted its leg, and Jesus dismounted and healed the injury with his healing hands, praying to God. The spell suggests that the reader does the same and puts his faith in God, Jesus, and the Holy Ghost.

## A Spell to Cast a Curse

A Scandinavian ritual for casting a curse onto an enemy involves a piece of paper, a pen, and a small box. The spellcaster writes the person's name to be cursed on the paper and then recites an incantation over the paper. This should include any personal details and the reason for the casting of the curse. Include what the curse should be, for example, bad luck, illness, or for their relationship to fail, before sealing the paper in the box. Take the box to a well or dig a hole in the garden. Put the box in the hole or cast it into the well while repeating the incantation you used when writing the person's name. Walk away and wait for the results.

## How to Lift a Curse

Are you constantly getting dumped in relationships? Have you lost your job for no discernible reason? Are you constantly fighting illness or weight fluctuations? Maybe you have a hex or curse placed on you. If you think that someone has set a hex on you, follow the spell below to remove it:

**What You Need to Do Is:**

- Take a piece of strong paper or wax parchment and write down what you know about the hex. Who may have cast it? How has it affected your life? Include as much detail as you can.
- Add three tsp. of Himalayan salt
- Fold the paper until it forms a bundle. Tie the end with a string
- Make the bundle into a pendant and wear it around your neck for three days
- On the fourth day, untie the bundle and sprinkle the salt into running water, especially from natural sources like a river or the rain
- Burn the paper and string and bury the ashes
- Now, wear a crystal around your neck for nine days to heal the damage to your system the hex may have caused

Congratulations, you are now hex and curse-free!

## Success Spells

What is success? More money, a better job, or a healthy relationship? Success means something different to everyone, and these spells from the black books of Scandinavia will help you improve your life generally and raise your level of success significantly.

## Create a Talisman to Wear

**What You Need:**

- A purple candle
- A green candle

- A personal sigil or talisman (you can use a cross, a crystal, a star, or a crescent symbol, whatever you feel speaks to you)
- A chain

Create a sacred space by cleansing with sage or blessed water, then place the two candles opposite each other. Light both the candles and stand in-between them with your sigil in your right hand. Lift the purple candle with your right hand and walk slowly toward the green candle. Place the purple candle next to the green one and recite a phrase that states your intention. Something like "I embrace and welcome success and happiness into my life," then attach the chain to the sigil and swing it between the flames.

Stop swinging when you feel your talisman is fully loaded and let the candles burn down naturally. Bury the wax in the garden and bless the space with a prayer. Wear the talisman whenever you feel the need for extra luck and success. Remember to reload this energy monthly and increase the potency by using the full moon to create extra magic powers.

## Luck Spell

If you are feeling down because things aren't going your way, don't worry. We can change all that with magic. This spell is a simple ritual using household goods. In the black book, many spells use ingredients that are simple to obtain because there weren't the resources available to practitioners that there are today. We only need to open our smartphones, and we can access all kinds of magical ingredients, but that wasn't true back then.

**What You Need:**

- Vinegar, apple cider, white wine, or classic will do
- A representation of yourself, a picture, a personal piece of jewelry, or a lock of hair
- Two white candles
- Sea salt, Himalayan is best
- White dish

If you know the day you were born, then perform the spell on that day. If you don't, then perform it on Monday for added luck. Choose a time when you are alone and won't be disturbed.

Begin by placing the candles on a table or altar if you have one. Light them both and close your eyes. Stay still and silent for two minutes.

Bring your hands together and bow your head. Recite a phrase that speaks to your needs: "Bring me success and luck through the power of this ritual."

Place the representation of yourself on the white dish and wet it with the vinegar. Sprinkle salt on the vinegar and place the dish in front of the candles. Hold the candles until the wax drips on them, and then replace them on the table.

Blow out the candle and place your object in a dark space.

Wait for a week, and then take the object out of the dark. Take it with you wherever you go, and you'll be blessed with success and luck.

## Love Spells

Witchcraft and trolldom are all about changing your life and making it better. Giving your love life a boost is a popular way to use spells and potions, so if you feel you are missing love and lust, try these spells adapted from the black book for modern times.

**What You Need:**

- Two candles, one white and one red
- Red ribbon
- Two pieces of paper and a pen
- Rose oil
- Red or pink cushion or cloth
- Fireproof dish or ashtray

Create a sacred space with a calm atmosphere and seat yourself on the cloth or cushion. Set up the two candles and join the bases with a red ribbon. Anoint the candles with the rose oil and write your name and the person you desire on the two pieces of paper.

Once the candles are lit, say your incantation. "I ask the universe for a union that will be loving and strong" or something that reflects your desires. Light both pieces of paper and let them burn in the fireproof dish. Let the candles burn down naturally, and then take the ashes outside and cast them into the wind.

Repeat the spell nine times for added strength and wait for the spell to attract the attention of your desired partner. The spell helps you feel open to love, increases your self-confidence, and enhances the magical forces of love.

## How to Strengthen the Love Your Partner Has for You

Do you have a partner but feel the relationship is imbalanced? Do you want to turn up the heat in your relationship and make sure you both feel the same way? Try this powerful love spell to get things heated with your partner:

**What You Need:**

- Two red candles
- A silver chain
- Love spell oil with rosemary rose and vanilla essential oil
- Toothpick for carving

Create your sacred space and perform the spell when the new moon is in the sky. Take the toothpick and carve your name in one candle and your partner's name in the other. Wrap the silver chain around them and place them on a table or altar. Light them while reciting this incantation or one you have made up yourself, "This spell will call your heart to join mine in the realm of love. As these candles burn, we clear the way for love to blossom and grow."

## Attract a Lost Love Back into Your Life

Why did you break up with someone you still love? If one of you cheated or significant issues caused the breakup, then walk away. This spell is designed to help when you have split with someone for reasons that seemed important at the time but are ridiculous. If insecurities and arguments drove you apart, try this healing spell to make the negative energies disappear:

**What You Need:**

- Two large white candles
- A purple candle

- Peppermint oil
- Sage for burning
- Rose incense stick

Cleanse the space with a sage smudge and then sit in the space while meditating. Remember all the enjoyable times you had with your partner and the laughs and love you shared. Now picture your future. The two of you are growing old and having a family or traveling the world. See yourself and your partner aging and loving each other through the future times.

Take the two white candles and name them, one with your name and the other with your ex-partner. Sprinkle peppermint oil on the candles and then light them, saying, "This candle is my Divine essence," and then the other saying, "This candle is (insert name of ex-partner" their Divine essence."

Light the purple candle, place it in front of the two white candles, and let it burn cleanly. Close your eyes and imagine the future once more filled with love and harmony. Now picture the conflicts you had disappearing with the smoke from the purple candle. Say something like, "We didn't know our love would suffer. We meant no harm. Let it be." Blow out all the candles and leave the space.

## Witchcraft Tips for Beginners

The black book may be dedicated to Scandinavian magic from centuries ago, but the issues it deals with are just as relevant today. Love, luck, and success are important, and sometimes you must cast a hex to get revenge. The main thing to remember is to do no actual harm. If you do, you may experience the power of a three-fold return. This means that if you wish harm to someone, it will be returned to you three times over.

Use magic to do good things and bring positivity to your life. Follow these simple rules to make your witchcraft safe and effective.

- **Learn from various sources.** Witchcraft is subjective and should reflect your beliefs, so don't follow instructions rigidly. Take the teachings of others and make them personal. Beginners can be wary about straying from the path regarding spells, but if you are careful and respect the craft, you'll be fine.

- **Write down your experiences**. The black book or the Cyprianus tradition is the perfect example of why written records are so important. Without records, witchcraft would have died out generations ago. Create a Book of Shadows or your own grimoire to record your progress and note your growth.
- **Leave the fear behind**. Don't let fear hold you back; remember why you are doing your magic. How did you feel when you first started thinking about magic? Excited and filled with wonder? Become experiential and practice your craft regularly, so you become more masterful, and it becomes part of your everyday life.
- **Experiment with the craft**. Try new tools and practices that appeal to your personality. Witchcraft is all about embracing nature and trying innovative ideas. As you experiment, you'll be drawn to certain parts of the craft, let that natural attraction influence your choices, and go with the flow. Your inner self is very rarely wrong, so trust your gut and let yourself experience new techniques.
- **Don't worry about failure**. Not everything will work; failure is just part of the learning process. Don't be put off by spells that don't work. Try alternative ingredients and techniques. Practice makes perfect; even the most seasoned witches don't know everything and can get it wrong.
- **Don't overspend on tools and altars**. When you see popular witches and practitioners on social media, they will often be surrounded by ornate altars and collections of paraphernalia. It is easy to become overawed and rush out to buy loads of stuff but remember, you have all the time in the world to build your collection. Homemade tools and wands are often more powerful and effective than shop-bought items so take your time and only buy things you feel drawn to.
- **Join communities**. There are lots of groups and online communities to choose from, and this doesn't mean joining a coven. If being part of a coven makes you nervous, then start with like-minded groups that practice Wicca or other pagan

and heathen practices. It takes time to become accustomed to talking freely about witchcraft, so choose a group you feel comfortable with. Stay safe and check out the resources before you give any details online and in person.

- **Accept the change**. Witchcraft and magic will change your life, and that is a fact. Don't be afraid. Nature and magic work together to connect you to the universe and improve your life. We are conditioned to believe that we aren't worthy of the better things in life, so you have to rise above those social dictates and accept your destiny.
- **Be culturally appropriate**. Some practitioners flaunt their beliefs and don't give a thought to other people. Not everyone believes, and that is their prerogative. It is also their right not to have witchcraft or paganism thrust into their lives. Don't force your ideas on other people, and don't wax lyrical about your new interest unless you are sure the other person is interested and won't be insulted or offended.

The black book is witchcraft from an age when it was normal to consult "crafty folk" to cure your ills. Modern practices can be adapted from these ancient ways to suit the life we lead today. Black magic has a bad reputation, but that was the fault of the early Christians. They were desperate to turn people away from paganism and make them believe it was evil. Most experts now recognize that the line between white and black magic is thin. Black magic is merely a different interpretation of white magic. If you are respectful and careful, it will work for you.

# Chapter 3: The Power of Herb Magic

Herbs are a staple part of our kitchens and are readily available. They have been used for generations as healing ingredients and home remedies. Most modern medicines seek to cure symptoms and rely on stronger drugs to deal with the causes of illness and underlying issues. Of course, modern medicine shouldn't be cast aside, but the ideal way to use herbology is to use it in conjunction with regular medicines to create a healthier way of treating ailments.

Humans are complicated organisms that are subject to attack by forces that mean to harm us. Germs, viruses, and other harmful forces need to be repelled, and we need to keep our bodies in a healthy form to combat the dangers we face daily. Herbology is the study of combining natural ingredients to form a strong defense against these forces and make us more stable and immune to their harmful properties.

Herbology is a magical way to keep yourself safe and feel better. Remember those special teas or hot drinks that your grandma made to make you feel special when you had a cold? Maybe a family recipe for a special soup when you were ill? Chances are that the herbs included in them were added by someone who knew their herbal magic and how to combine them to make a magical remedy passed down through the family for generations.

In this next section, we will uncover the properties that herbs bring to magic and when they should be used. Three specific types of magic are covered, and a list of herbs can increase the potency of your spells and remedies.

## Protection Spells

### Acacia

Also known as Wattle or Mimosa, this herb grows in warm climates and is partly used to anoint sacred spaces and create healing baths. The young leaves and flowers are edible and can be used in teas and potions. Use this herb to break hexes and curses and consecrate your magic tools.

### African Violet

Violets can be found growing everywhere and are a great ingredient for making teas and syrups, but African violets can cause indigestion and should be used solely to protect the home when burned as incense. Use it to power your amulets and wear them around your neck.

### Alder

This herb is found in trees growing near the riverbanks and is harvested by collecting the catkins that hang from the branches. The herb is filled with protein and astringent and can be used as a strong anti-inflammatory ingredient. Use in potions to create weather magick and influence decision-making. The herb is associated with the protection of the newly deceased and is often used in teas at funerals.

### Aloe Vera

This plant grows wild in tropical and arid places but can be purchased in many forms from suitable sources. It has been used for medicinal purposes for over 6,000 years and is a handy part of your magical life. Add the leaves to salads or use the gel to enhance teas or as a dressing for dips. Water containing aloe can be bought from your supermarket, which will help you balance your body heat when the temperatures soar.

### Althea Root

This powerful herb grows near lakes and marshes and is also known as marshmallow root. It can be consumed raw to aid coughs and colds or can be steeped in water to create a tea that cures dry mouth and protects against ulcers. It can be used as a poultice to treat burns and wounds or soothe skin irritation.

**Angelica**

This decorative hardy herb is found in colder climates and has multiple healing properties. It protects the body from toxins and increases blood circulation. It has been used for centuries to treat menstruation problems and is often called female ginseng. It is believed the name originates from the tale of a monk who received the herb from the heavens to help him treat people suffering from the plague. Use it to flavor foods and drinks with a smoky musky taste and aroma for daily use.

**Basil**

**Basil**

*https://pixabay.com/images/id-1248955/*

This common herb can be grown everywhere, and even the smallest pot will yield a healthy amount. Use it to drive away hostile spirits and sprinkle it in your bath for a magical protective shield. Add it to the final cooking stage to keep the herb fresh and effective. In Europe, basil is used to create holy water utilized in the church due to its strong protective qualities.

**Bergamot**

Wild bergamot is found in North America and is used in gardens to attract butterflies and bees to the area. It reduces cholesterol and relieves stress. Use the herb in its natural form or use the essential oil to flavor teas and potions. Add to your remedies to alleviate joint pain and increase mental alertness. Bergamot oil used in aromatherapy is a powerful way to relieve anxiety and protect the user from stress.

### Black Cohosh

A Woodland herb native to North America, black cohosh is used to alleviate women's estrogen-related symptoms like night sweats, hot flashes, and other menopausal and menstrual conditions. It also relieves headaches and is a powerful aid in improving digestion function. Use it in teas or potions, or take it as a capsule.

### Black Pepper

This common household condiment is also a powerful magic ingredient. Mix it with salt to scatter around the home for protection or to season your food. Burn black pepper for a powerful smudge or use it as incense to clear the home from negative energies.

### Boneset

Grown in North America, this is a lesser-known herb of the magnoliids family of plants. It has been used for generations by Native North Americans to treat respiratory conditions and ease fevers. Mix with peppermint leaves and elder herb to make a tea to guard against allergies, viruses, and colds. It will strengthen your immunity and make your bones stronger.

### Burdock

Grown in Europe and Asia, this herb is a powerhouse of antioxidants and removes toxins from the blood. It is rich in fiber and helps regulate blood pressure and digestion. The natural properties of burdock help the liver function well and promote flawless skin. It can be added to food and drink in dried form, or the roots can be eaten raw.

### Calamint

Found growing in the temperate regions of Europe, calamint clears any airway infections and stops digestive cramps and convulsions. It is an effective congestion relief, and you can use the flowers, stems, and leaves depending on your needs. Use in tea or to flavor foods.

**Caraway**

This herb is found in Asia, Europe, and Africa and is a relative of the carrot. In ancient times herbalists used the seeds to relieve digestive gas and as a general tonic for digestion.

**Catnip**

This aromatic herb is found in central Europe and has been used in food preparation for generations. Its leaves are great for herbal teas, and the herb is also added to tonic wines and liquor. Mix the leaves with your salad for a tasty protective way to aid sleep or create a calming effect on the nerves.

**Chia**

One of the more modern "superfoods," chia seeds, have been used in herbology for generations. Eat them in a salad for nutrition, or use their magical properties to protect yourself from gossip and slander.

**Chives**

Another common herb that has strong protective properties. It was used in exorcisms and banishing to keep the subject safe from evil. Use these properties and add chives to your diet and your magic potions.

**Cinquefoil**

This herb is prolific in Europe and grows easily in most gardens. Use it to treat swellings in the mouth and blisters or ulcers. It is a powerful laxative and, as a tea, it is used to treat colds and flu by reducing inflammation. Used externally, it can reduce the pain of insect stings, wounds, and acne. Crush the roots and flowers, add them to a jar of vodka and leave them in a dark space for ten days. Filter the liquid through a cloth and use it as a daily supplement to strengthen your immune system. This potion is more potent than the tea, so a teaspoon a day will suffice.

**Cloves**

Sourced from Asia and South America, cloves will help you dispel negativity and stop gossip. They are an effective pain relief method and have been used to ease toothache for thousands of years. Add to meat dishes and curries to promote health and protection for your immune system.

**Comfrey**

This is a prolific herb and can be found in most environments. It is effective in curing skin issues and is also used as a muscle relaxant. Its magical uses include travel protection; a sachet in your luggage will protect you from theft and other issues.

**Devils Bit**

This ingredient is a rare herb from Europe that can bring love and protection and increase your chances of romance. Use it as a tea or as a tincture to treat bruises and wounds. Traditional folklore says that the plant's appearance looks like the head has been bitten off because the Devil was so jealous of the plant's magical properties that he wanted to deprive humankind of its virtues.

**Devils Claw**

Native to South America this herb resembles a gnarled hook-like hand which led to its rather ominous name. It is used to treat gout and other inflammatory issues, and, in magic, it is a powerful protection ingredient. Hang sachets around your home to keep you safe from evil spirits.

**Dogwood**

This herb is an intensely powerful way to guard your journals. Use it to protect your book of shadows or grimoires.

**Elder**

Elder is a prolific plant found in most climates and is the source of the elder herb, which is especially effective when treating colds and flu. In potions, it helps protect from viral infections and makes the immune system stronger. Ground elder can help cure gout and other joint pain.

**Eucalyptus**

This herb is sourced from Australia and Tasmania and includes over five hundred species of plants. It can be used topically to treat acne and skin complaints and provides a healing balm for burns and other wounds. Inhaling the oil helps respiratory issues and promotes relaxation. The plant should never be consumed fresh, but the dried leaves can be used in tea to decrease blood pressure and relieve anxiety and stress. Its eucalyptol oil is a natural insect repellant and can be used to keep your home bug free.

**Fennel**

Originally from Europe, this hardy perennial herb can now be found worldwide. It is a member of the carrot family and is full of flavor. The seeds can be added to potions to provide anti-bacterial properties and nutrition. The seeds can be used to make a tea that helps relieve anemia, constipation, and wind. They are also delicious when roasted and served as a side dish.

**Figwort**

Found throughout the Northern hemisphere, figwort has been used in herbal medicine for generations and is a powerful part of your herb collection. Hundreds of different species are used to treat skin conditions like psoriasis and eczema. It can be added to potions to stimulate the heart and acts as a laxative. If you have a heart condition, avoid this herb as it can make it worse and affect the rhythm of your heart.

**Fleabane**

A common medicinal wildflower, this handy plant can be sued to treat urogenital diseases like gonorrhea and urinary tract infections. Its Mexican cousin can be used to treat toothache and other oral issues. In magic potions, it is a source of protection against negative energy and is used in exorcisms.

**Galangal**

A member of the ginger family, galangal is found in Asia and is a staple part of Thai cuisine. In traditional medicinal practices, it is used to treat dysentery, skin conditions, and bad breath. It increases the sperm count and is used in potions to boost fertility.

**Garlic**

A staple part of most kitchen supplies, garlic is both practical and one of the more magical plants available. It famously repels vampires and is used to purify spaces and objects. Use it to protect your home and your sacred spaces and carry it when you feel exposed to other people's negativity.

**Ginger**

Another common part of your kitchen supplies is adding ginger to your potions to bring good health and protection. Dried ginger can be added to mojo bags for extra magical potency.

### Ginseng

Found in South China, ginseng varieties are now available in the USA and can be used in magic to promote sexual potency and performance. It helps memory and promotes magical connections by improving cognitive forces. Medicinally it also reduces the metabolism and boosts the cells to fight infections.

### Heather

Traditionally used by Romany people to bring good luck and fortune, heather is a common plant with magical properties. Burn a smudge stick of heather and fern to bring rain and hang it around the house to bring peace and harmony. Carry it on your person to protect yourself from attacks and sexual crimes.

### Juniper

This magical berry is one of the oldest trees on earth. It is found on every continent and can survive the harshest climates and lack of water. It represents wisdom and perseverance and can promote raised vibrations and open your third chakra when used as a smudge. Carry the berries to protect you while you travel and use them in a bath to attract love and new relationships.

### Lady Slipper

Found across the northern hemisphere, these hardy orchids are added to potions to promote sleep. It is quite expensive and should only be included in your herbal collection if you are experiencing difficulties with sleeping.

### Lavender

Another common herb, it is said that burning lavender is a powerful way to promote restful auras. Burn the flowers and scatter the ashes to bring peace to your area.

### Mandrake

Another traditional herb used for centuries, mandrake, is found in southern Europe and North Africa. Its roots look like human genitalia; they help the wearer attract new sexual partners when carried. Slip a mandrake root beneath your pillow to encourage fertility and conception. Mandrake oil is used to anoint candles to increase their potency.

**Marigold**

The common garden flower should be added to baths to bring confidence and protection while you sleep.

**Marshmallow Root**

This is a slippery root used for medicinal properties for generations. It soothes inflammation, and in potions, it helps to cure colds and sore throats. It originates in Africa but can be found in herbal supply outlets worldwide. The Ancient Greeks used marshmallow root to create a balm for insect stings, while the Romans used it as a laxative.

**Mint**

Simple to grow and incredibly powerful, mint is a protective herb that can be added to most dishes and teas to create a tasty magical force.

**Nutmeg**

Another kitchen staple sprinkles it on green candles in spells for money or prosperity. It gives the wearer protection when used to make amulets or added to mojo bags.

**Orris Root**

This hybrid plant is used in perfumes and scents but in magic; it is better known for its drawing power. It can draw toxins out both physically and spiritually and is also used to promote dreamwork and divination powers. It has powerful connections to the female arts and is used as an attraction herb in rituals concerning passion and romance. Medicinally, it boosts the nervous system and is also effective in oral health.

**Pimpernel**

Part of the burnet plant family, this brilliant scarlet flower grows wild and can be harvested easily. It has a reputation for its supposed narcotic quality, but wild pimpernel won't contain anything that will alter your state of mind. The dried leaves brewed in a tea will provide a carminative relief for wind and aid any other digestive issues.

**Red Clover**

Originally sourced in Europe, the plant has been naturalized in most regions and can be found in most countries. It is used to treat skin conditions and menstruation ailments and to purify the liver and digestive tract. In magic, it is also used to purify areas, especially when used in a smudge. Red clover tea helps stimulate the brain and reduces anxiety, and adding mint and hibiscus brings added wisdom.

### Rowan

Known as the sacred witch tree, rowan has featured in magical rituals and practices since the time of the druids. In Norse mythology, the first woman was crafted from the bark of the rowan, and it is the preferred wood for creating magical talismans and runes. They are planted in graveyards to protect the dead, and their berries are used in protection spells. They contain slightly toxic acids, so they must be cooked before they are ready to digest.

### Rue

Found in the Mediterranean, this herb is known as the queen of herbs. It is used in magic to protect the users from evil and lift curses and hexes. It is added to potions that are used for purification and can be added to baths for spiritual cleansing. It is used in lovers' incense when mixed with sandalwood and lavender.

### Sandalwood

Another common herb should be scattered around the home to protect and purify the space. It is used in exorcism rituals and will help you banish negativity and evil.

### Spearmint

Use spearmint leaves or oil in a bath for strength, vitality, and protection.

### St. John's Wort

This prolific wildflower has been used in magic since the Middle Ages to protect households from evil spirits and witches. Today we know it is a healthy way to lift the spirits and ease addictive tendencies. Use it in house purifications or potions to keep the body healthy and rested.

### Thistle

The common thistle is prickly and can cause skin irritation. Use it carefully to make tea for protection or hang it in the house to ward off negativity.

### Witch Hazel

Found in North America, Japan, and China, this plant is a strong astringent and can be used to clean wounds and calm stings. Wiccan spells include witch hazel to create an emotional balance and purge the mind of troubling energy.

These herbs and plants give you a base to work with since we always need protection when performing witchcraft. Other elements are added to give meaning to potions and spells to create a mixture of magical properties to enhance your knowledge.

These individual herbs will signal your intent and bring strength and power to your work:

## Love, Passion, Sex, and Romance

### Adam and Eve's Roots

Native to North America, these roots come in different shapes that resemble male and female genitalia. In traditional spells, the male will take the female root, and the female will take the male root to attract members of the other sex. Of course, modern magic works just as well in same-sex and polygamous relationships so just adapt the ritual to the needs of the people involved. Carry both roots in a magic bag to attract a proposal or new love.

### Black Cohosh

This common plant yields natural elements to help sleep and fertility. It can be bought dried from herbal resources and used to make tea and boost your chances of attracting love.

### Caraway

These seeds are often found in cakes, but in magic, they are used to bind lovers to you and stop them from straying or cheating.

### Cardamon

Sourced in India and the subcontinents, this tasty herb is used in curries and other spicy dishes. In magic, it is a powerful ingredient in love and lust magic. Placed in a pouch with other Venus-related objects, it will attract love and passion.

### Chamomile

Use a restful bath to prepare yourself for new love and increased potency.

**Chili Pepper**

Also known as cayenne, this is another staple direct from your kitchen cupboard. This spicy herb is a sure-fire ingredient that adds heat to your love life and breaks hexes. Add it to your foods or use it in your potions to add spice and get your love muscles flexing.

**Elecampane**

Part of the sunflower family, it is native to Eurasia and is a powerful plant when performing magic to attract love. It was used in Ancient Greece as a tonic that enriched the blood and helped the heart function healthily.

**Evening Primrose**

Native Americans have used this North American wildflower for generations for performing magic. Use it in a bath to reveal your inner beauty or in spells that promote success and achieve your goals. Because it flowers at night, it works well with spells relating to moon magic and the goddess Diana.

**Laurel**

Native to Asia Minor, use this herb to decorate your altar, enhance psychic dreams, and reveal the name of your next true love. To keep a current love true, both of you should visit a laurel tree, choose a leaf, and split it in two. If you both keep hold of your half of the leaf, neither of you will be tempted to stray.

**Lovage**

Use in a bath to enhance your natural attractiveness and draw potential partners to your energy.

**Marjoram**

Another staple kitchen herb, just adding a few leaves will enhance any love spell, or you can just put it in your food.

**Myrtle**

One of the most powerful love herbs in your collection, it has been used for generations to decorate crowns for grooms and brides and to decorate marriage altars. It was reputedly the name used for women's genitalia back in Ancient Greece. Use it fresh or as an oil to boost love spells for intimacy and to strengthen connections.

**Parsley**

This kitchen staple can be worn in your shoe to make you more attractive to others.

**Periwinkle**

Grown in Madagascar, this pretty flower is essential in love spells and potions. Burn the dried leaves before having sex with your partner to intensify the experience.

**Quassia**

Originating in South America, this is a healthy herb used in herbal medicine, but in magic, it can ensure you keep your relationship. Simply take a lock of your hair and add one from your lover, burn the hair on some quassia chips and then keep the ashes safe to preserve the love you have for each other.

**Saffron**

This expensive and glorious spice can be used to make the blandest dish look and taste amazing. In magic, just a nip of saffron will do the same for your potions and spells, especially when you are conjuring passion and love.

**Sesame**

Another common herb adds to your spells to attract lust and success.

**Tonka Beans**

A popular ingredient in Hoodoo magic, Tonia beans are used to attract love and passion.

**Ylang Ylang**

Use the essential oil to enhance your sexual spells and bring the power of fairy magic to your work.

## Abundance Spells

**Basil**

Used to create new opportunities for financial success. Add to your spells for abundance, and when you cleanse your sacred space, add basil leaves to the hot water for prosperity.

**Comfrey**

This magic herb is commonly found in the wild and is often used to treat skin conditions. It brings strength to spells regarding real estate or property in magical terms. Carry some with you when you travel to keep yourself and your belongings safe.

**Fenugreek**

Burn the dried leaves to attract money and fertility. Place in a jar with protection herbs and add a small amount every day. As the jar fills, so will your bank account.

**Hollyhock**

This impressive bush should be grown near your home to attract wealth and prosperity to you and the occupants.

**Irish Moss**

A species of red algae that grows on rocks around the Atlantic part of Europe, this is a handy ingredient in abundance spells.

**Jobs Tears**

Asiatic grass is used in magic to represent luck when finding employment and money. Use the grass in lucky bags and bring good luck to your spells.

**Thyme**

Add to your bath to bring luck, prosperity, and a constant flow of money to your home.

Obviously, this list is just a few herbs and plants available for your crafting. Like traditional cooking, whenever you find a new ingredient, you will be tempted to add it to your spells. Also, you'll find your individual favorites and special herbs and plants that you can add to any mixture to make it personal.

Herbology is a never-ending learning curve, but don't let that make you feel overwhelmed. It is fun, providing you do your research and avoid poisonous ingredients. Keep yourself safe and enjoy your herbal experiments.

# Chapter 4: Cauldron Magic

The word cauldron conjures up an image of a gnarled old hag cackling as she stirs her potions in a large metal pot over an open flame. While this image may have been true centuries ago, most modern witches recognize the need to go with the times and use more modern pots to brew their potions. It is important to remember that whatever your cauldron or pot is made of could make it difficult to care for.

Cast iron pots can be a nightmare to keep clean even if they do look the part. Some herbs also react badly to iron, and this can make a potion go bad or even cause harm to the recipient. Fortunately, there are more modern materials that are more suited to potion brewing so let's look at the materials available depending on what your potions will be:

**Cast Iron**

**Cast iron cauldrons are traditionally used.**

*https://pixabay.com/images/id-3818908/*

The traditional pots look great and make your spells feel more authentic, and are great if you use them just for burning incense or herbs for cleansing purposes. You can buy a relatively inexpensive model from online resources or search thrift shops for a more traditional iron pot. Dutch ovens are another way to convert modern cooking utensils into a tool for witchcraft and are easily sourced. Remember that cleaning your cauldron is essential, and iron models can be more labor-intensive.

**Ceramic**

Cauldrons made from ceramics can be beautiful, lighter to use, and easier to clean. They look great on your kitchen shelves, and you can buy them with personal decorations to make your work more personalized. Ceramic models are generally less expensive than metal pots, and you can buy them easily from most retail sources. Don't forget that ceramic pots come in all shapes and sizes, and even a teacup can be used for smaller potions or burning incense. True witches care more about the end result than their tools' aesthetics.

**Glass**

This is a controversial material for some witches, but many more are beginning to appreciate the aesthetic value of glass cauldrons. The sheer wonder of watching your potion brew from all angles has persuaded even the most traditional witches to use them for their potions. Make sure the glass is heat-proof and the pot is fairly robust. Some glass pots are only meant for decoration and won't withstand more vigorous stirring or being heated and cooled.

When you choose a cauldron, remember to choose one with a lid if needed and a handle if you plan to take your magic with you on your travels. Don't use your cauldron for everyday cooking, as you risk contamination and lowering your work's magical properties. Like your other tools, the cauldron is an extension of you and shouldn't be used by others. It isn't part of your household goods and should be kept for special occasions.

## What Are Potions?

Quite simply, a potion is a liquid made with magical intentions. It can be used as a drink or for topical use. It can also be used to bless items and cleanse both physical and spiritual areas. They can also be referred to as elixirs, infusions, balms, or magical balms. No matter what you call it, the power of potions is a combination of the ingredients combined and the ritual of preparation.

## How to Start Your Potion

Remember that just like a regular cooking area, the space you are using needs to be clean, but even more so in the process of magic potions. The area you are using should be physically clean and spiritually free from debris. Create a cleansing smoke by burning sage or your favorite herb and pass all your ingredients and tools through the smoke to cleanse them. Take the burning sage to the four points of the room and say a few healing words to make the effect more intense. Banish negative energy and make the space feel grounded and sacred.

## Magic Potion-Based Liquids

When you start creating potions, knowing where to start can be daunting, so beginners and experts recognize the importance of a base liquid. Witches often avoid potions because they seem complicated and can easily go wrong. Think of creating portions the same way you approach your ordinary cooking skills, which involve a recipe that can be adjusted to suit your needs. How many times have you taken a well-loved recipe and made it your own? The same principle applies to magic. Once the basics are covered, you can change the potions to suit you and your magic.

## Choose a Base Liquid

When making a potion, choosing the base liquid that suits the spell you are creating is important. Here is a list of some basic liquids that work well with herbs, crystals, and other magic ingredients.

- **Water:** Perhaps the most accessible source of liquid but also the most versatile. Tap water works, but where's the imagination in that? Try infusing your water with crystals or leaving it in the moon's light to become "moon water" or infusing it with sunlight. Try natural sources to bring the power of nature to your spells and use river or spring water. If your spell involves traveling, then use seawater to bring in the power of nature's mighty oceans. Remember to use filtered or bottled water if your spell is going to be consumed.

- **Fruit or Vegetable Juice:** Who says you can't have healthy potions? Use bright-colored juices to add a splash of flavor and vitamins to your potions. The magical properties of the colors and the magical quality of the place where it was grown could be used.
- **Red, White, or Rose Wine:** When you use alcohol, you need to be careful if you share your potion but if it is for your own use, then go for it. Wine is a great base for potions and works well with herbs and other natural ingredients. Remember, if you're heating wine, the alcohol content will often be dissipated, and the liquid will lose its potency.
- **Natural Sources:** If you can drink it, you can use it in a potion, providing it isn't too processed. If you are creating a potion that will be drunk, then your base can also be a drinkable liquid like tea or coffee. There are so many natural alternatives you can use, like plant-based milk or yogurt, that the choices are both endless and healthy.
- **Oils:** Oils make the perfect base if your potion is for topical use. Almond or other nut oils are easily purchased from local sources, making a smoother and easy-to-apply potion. While some oils can be expensive, plain vegetable oil is a cheaper alternative, readily found in most kitchen cupboards.

Now you have the basics. A clean area, your chosen cauldron, a glass jar to keep the finished product in, and your athame to chop the ingredients. You also need a heat source when cooking your potion and relative safety equipment when using a naked flame. Your ritual must speak to all four of the elements to invoke the power of nature, so the heat source is your connection to the fire, the base liquid is water, the steam is an air connection, and your ingredients are linked to the earth.

State your intentions as you prepare for your ritual. Thank the elements for their daily presence in your life. Ask the spirits to join you in your work and encompass their energy into what you are doing. Spells always work better with well-stated intentions, and potions are no different. Positive statements will put you in the right frame of mind and help you focus.

## Magical Potions

Now you have the knowledge of herbs and plants and your cauldron, it is time to dive into the magical world of potions. This section will explore some simple beginners' potions and then progress to more complex mixtures. Throughout history, potions have been produced to cure all manner of ailments, from simple illness to finding love, securing immortality, or curing the plague. In the medieval ages, doctors and trained apothecaries were mostly male and required payment for their services, while those who couldn't afford to pay for their potions turned to local wise women to administer their homemade potions and salves, performing prayers and chants to increase their efficiency. These were early forms of witchcraft, and they were administered to members of society who were impoverished.

Scandinavians especially featured love potions known as Philters, which were documented in the Norse poem "The Lay of Gudrun" from the Poetic Edda. Norse mythology is filled with tales of potions, salves, elixirs, and other magical mixtures that influence others.

Here are some modern takes on trolldom and Norse potions. Feel free to add or change the recipes to suit your needs, ingredients, and intentions. Some of these potions are made from ingredients in your kitchen cupboards, while others will take more effort.

## Self-Love Potion

The best way to make your work effective is to believe in it. The ingredients, the method, and most of all, the person doing it, yes, that's you, so making your first potion a self-love mixture makes perfect sense.

## The Hibiscus Love Potion

This simple herbal tea has no caffeine content and can be consumed both heated and cold. Make a batch to keep in the fridge for when you need a boost of self-confidence.

**What You Need:**

- Hibiscus tea
- Sugar
- Mint leaves
- Pink candle
- Small metal container
- Cup
- Water

Dress your altar with a candle and a white cloth. Turn off all your electronics and keep them out of your sacred area. Play soothing music or just enjoy the silence. Heat the water in the metal container with the candle flame while you recite the following "I am loved, I am worthy of that love, and I accept it with the power of the universe. Bring me a wave of inner peace, and let me rid myself of negativity and darkness while I let the light of the world fill me up."

Add the tea and water to your cup and sweeten it to taste. Sprinkle the mint and drink after it has brewed. As you sip the tea, imagine your best life, that job you know you are worthy of, the partner you know you deserve, and see yourself surrounded by the love of people around you.

## A Healing Potion for Low-Level Ailments or to Boost Energy

This is a simple brew that will make you feel energized and drive those nagging ailments away.

**What You Need:**

- 2 small pieces of willow bark
- 1 tbsp. vanilla extract
- 1 tbsp. apple juice
- A pinch of sage
- Pinch of rosemary
- 2 drops of lemon juice
- Water

Dress your altar with a light blue cloth and place the ingredients in your cauldron. Add your preferred base liquid. We have used water in this example and boiled the liquid. As the water boils, recite this mantra "Healing liquid be my balm, stop the pain and heal the harm." Once the liquid has cooled, pour it into a cup and sip the tea while imagining all the pain leaving your body. Imagine the white light filling you with energy and excitement for what the day holds for you, and picture the fatigue leaving your body and floating away into the ether.

## Healing Potion Made with Ingredients from Your Kitchen

This potion is especially effective for colds, sore throats, laryngitis, and menstrual issues

## Cold and Flu Potion

**What You Need:**

- Ginger, either dried or ground root
- 1 tbsp. lemon juice
- 1 tbsp. Manuka honey
- A pinch of cinnamon
- Brown sugar
- Water or lemon tea

This can be brewed on your altar or created in your kitchen on the stove. Add all the ingredients to a pot and let it simmer for ten minutes while you recite the following: "Magic potion, do your thing, clear my throat so I can sing, let your magic soothe my soul and make me feel whole forever." Once the potion has cooled, sweeten it and drink whenever needed.

## Protection Potion to Keep Negative Energy at Bay

This potion can be ingested to keep you safe or used to sprinkle around your home for added protection. It can be bottled and used for up to three months after brewing.

**What You Need:**

- Jasmin tea bag
- 1 tbsp. Manuka honey
- 2 cloves
- 1 tbsp. lemon juice
- 3 bay leaves
- Sprinkle of black pepper
- Water
- Cup
- Sugar

Dress your altar in gold or red cloth and decorate with your favorite crystals or gemstones. Add anything you feel represents your favorite parts of your life, like your house keys, jewelry, or pictures of your family or friends.

Place the cauldron on the altar, add the ingredients (except the sugar), and repeat the following prayer. "I call upon the divine to make me feel safe. Bless me with your all-encompassing energy and shield me from harm. Be my guardian and give me the strength to shield others and myself."

Now take the cauldron to your kitchen and brew the potions. Use it to consecrate your home or drink it depending on your needs. Imagine a bright white dome surrounding all the things you love, and then picture the negative forces being repelled into the darkness.

## Alcoholic Potions Just for Adults

## Raspberry Honey Potion

This boozy potion is to cleanse and purify your energy and attract new love or friends

**What You Need:**

- Raspberry vodka
- Raspberry tea
- Hibiscus tea

- 1 tsp caramel syrup
- Lemon juice
- Honey
- Peppermint cordial
- Ice
- Cocktail shaker or cauldron

You can make the process more magical by dressing your altar in pink, yellow, or white cloths and a couple of candles, but this potion really is just about the end product. Add all the ingredients to your chosen receptacle and either stir or shake. Add the ice as you mix or put it into a glass to cool the liquid. As you sip your potion, thank the gods, goddesses, and the universe for your good fortune and thank them for their interest in you and your life.

## A Love Potion Based on Wine

This is a tasty potion designed for long hot summer days filled with the promise of romance and the joy of new love

**What You Need:**

- Wine, you can use white or rose
- Fresh peaches
- Raspberries
- Vanilla pods
- Sprig of mint
- Ice
- Glass

Fill a glass with ice and add the wine. As you add the other ingredients, ask the heavens to send you positive energy and a vision of your perfect partner. Once the potion has been stirred and chilled, sip it slowly and imagine how the two of you will look in the future. Thank the goddess of love and romance for her help.

## Alcohol-Based Sleep Potion

Take this warming potion before you go to bed; it will help you fall asleep and promote positive dreams. This comforting potion will make you feel drowsy and warm as you fall into a deep slumber.

**What You Need:**

- 1 shot of dark rum
- Cinnamon
- Dark sugar
- Water or milk, depending on your taste
- An orange candle
- Lavender essence
- Cauldron
- Cup

Dress your altar with muted color cloth and place the orange candle on the surface. Put the rum, cinnamon, sugar, and water/milk in your cauldron on the stove and bring it to a boil before letting it simmer for two minutes. Bring the cauldron to the altar, light the candle, and sprinkle the essence on your altar as you pour the potion into a cup. Recite the following "Take me to the land of rest and let my sleep be the best, help me dream of past and present, and show me how to be ready for the future."

Drink the potion and let your eyes droop as you imagine the future filled with love and success.

## Wine-Based Potion for Love and Lust

This sexy potion will bring a romantic boost to even the most tired love life. Make a cauldron full and keep it bottled for when you want a repeat session with your loved one.

**What You Need:**

- A bottle of sweet red or white wine
- 5 fresh basil leaves
- 6 red rose petals
- 3 cloves

- 4 apple seeds
- 2 drops of pomegranate essence
- 2 oz. raspberry juice
- A large piece of ginseng root
- Cauldron
- Tea cloth for straining
- Glass jar with a sealable top

Decorate your altar with red and white cloths, and then add white quartz, moonstone, and garnet to the table. Add all the ingredients to the cauldron and take it to the kitchen. Decorate the area you are working in with colored candles and tea lights. Stir the mixture over low heat and say, "I give this wine to show my love and hope they find it tasty, bring my love into my life and make their arrival hasty." As it cools, thank the goddess of love Freya for her ministrations and then bottle it. Keep it in the fridge until you find the person you feel is worthy of your love.

## Other Regular Potions for Everyday Life

Strictly speaking, coffee and other daily beverages are not tied to Norse traditions but are part of modern Scandi and Nordic life today. Adapt your potions and rituals to include them, so you don't miss a trick when it comes to introducing magic into your routine.

## Daily Coffee Potion

Have you ever thought of the magical properties of coffee? In the olden days, it was referred to as "Satan's brew," so its ties with magic go back further than you think. What do you feel when you have coffee? Happier, energized, comforted, or inspired? Coffee has multiple uses apart from being a drink. It energizes our system and boosts energy so remember to treat the humble java with the respect it deserves and keep it in your kitchen store.

## Use Brewed Coffee for These Magical Uses

- Remove blockages by sipping the liquid or bathing in it. Add some herbs or essential oils to a bath to remove negativity from your aura and your environment.
- Remove a curse by using coffee as a base liquid for a protection spell, or drink it while you repeat the source of the curse to ensure you dispel the energy behind the hex.
- Dispel negative spirits by washing your sacred space with a diluted solution of coffee and sage.
- Improve your luck by stirring the coffee vigorously to create bubbles and then using a spoon to scoop them up and drink.
- Connect with the deities by offering them a tasty cappuccino or espresso. They are just as fond of their brew as you are and will be pleased to share your daily routine.

## Money Potion

Use this potion to attract wealth and financial success and improve any business you conduct. The potion can be drunk cold or hot and stored in a jar for up to a week.

**What You Need:**

- 4 cups of water
- 2 sticks of cinnamon
- 4 cloves
- 1 tsp all spice powder
- 2 sprigs of fresh mint
- 2 tsp. brown sugar

Dress your altar in green and gold cloth and light a white candle anointed with your favorite oil. Place three-dollar bills on the altar. Take your cauldron to the kitchen and boil the water and all the other ingredients except the fresh mint for five minutes. Cover the cauldron and let the mixture steep for ten minutes off the heat. Repeat the following "Money and cash are nice to own; they make me happy and fill my soul if the universe wills it to bring that wealth and love to me."

Take the liquid and add the fresh mint. Leave it to cool before straining it and serving it with ice or as a reheated beverage. Feel the emotion you will experience as you receive your rewards while you sip the potion. After you have finished, thank the spirits for their help. For further strength, sprinkle the potion on the dollar bills and leave them on your altar.

## Increased Focus Potion

Feeling a bit stressed and experiencing low energy levels? Are you struggling to focus on work or at home, or do you just want to empower your mind? Try this refreshing potion to bring energy to your aura and elevate your senses.

**What You Need:**

- 6 fresh lemons
- 4 cups of water
- A sprig of fresh rosemary
- Brown sugar
- Honey
- Lime juice
- Bay leaves
- Glass
- Ice

Make the basic juice by squeezing the lemons into three cups of water. As you squeeze, empower them by visualizing a smarter and sharper you after you have taken the potion. Imagine those awesome ideas you'll have and the positivity flowing from your mind. Set the juice aside to infuse with the rest of the ingredients.

On the stove, heat the remaining water with the rosemary, sugar, and honey. Let it boil for ten minutes until all the sugar has dissolved. Now let the mixture cool as you imagine the success you'll find in the future. That new job or the prospect of new experiences, let your senses become laser-focused on your future.

Add ice to a glass and pour in the lemon liquid. Remove the rosemary sprig and use the sweet liquid to enchant the lemony taste. Create a sweet elixir to promote your mental health and enjoy.

## Aphrodisiac Passion Potion

This potion is a powerful way to warm someone up and get them in the mood for love, but they are not miracle mixtures. They will not make someone who has no interest in you change their mind, but they will bring passion back to a relationship that may have gone flat.

## Bring the Heat Potion

**What You Need:**

- Sprig of rosemary
- ½ tsp thyme
- A pinch of sage
- A pinch of nutmeg
- 2 tsp mint tea leaves
- 3 cloves
- 3 rose petals
- 6 drops of lemon juice
- Water
- Picture of your loved one
- A piece of rose quartz

Set up your altar with red and pink cloths and light three white candles. Set the picture and the quartz in front of the middle white candles. Add the other ingredients to your cauldron and heat them over the candles, or take them into the kitchen and warm them on the stove.

As the mixture cools, repeat the following "Love and heat fill me with hope and love; let this tea bring the passion back to my love and me." Strain the liquid and sip it while you visualize the heat you two will bring to the bedroom.

These are just a few of the potions that can be made for different occasions. It would be impossible to list them all. Imagine asking for a list of every recipe in the world. You have your ingredients, you know the power they bring, and now you have the confidence to make your own magical potions, salves, and tinctures. Providing your ingredients are safe, your potions will be. Have fun and experiment with your workings; remember to note the recipes so you can add them to your grimoire or Book of Shadows when they work.

# Chapter 5: Magical Swords and Daggers

Norse trolldom is a place where fighting and battles are all part of life. The gods and goddesses fought hard, loved with passion, and used weapons to increase their chances of winning. Today we recognize that the most powerful weapons in our arsenal are intelligence, knowledge, morality, and truth. However, this doesn't mean that the historical weapons of trolldom aren't relevant. They show the passion behind the stories, beliefs, and the force of nature that drives the magic. Plus, the stories are meant to be dramatic and filled with mighty battles, including some of the most fantastic weapons crafted by mystical creatures and endowed with magical powers.

# Weapons from Mythology and Norse Practices

## The Trident

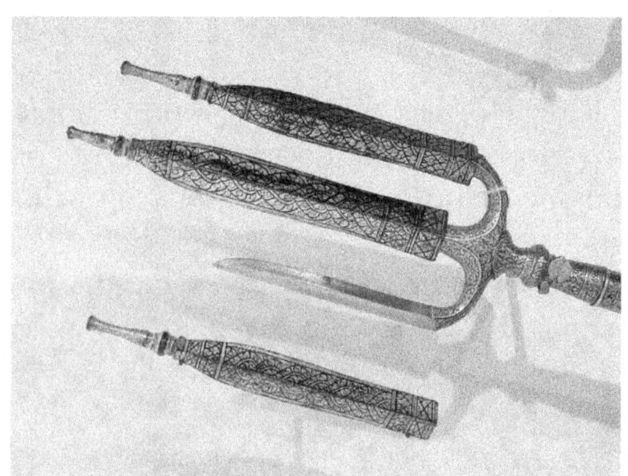

**Tridents are usually weapons of sea gods.**
*https://commons.wikimedia.org/wiki/File:Trident,_Burmese,_18th_century.JPG*

The three-pronged spear is named from the Latin words for three teeth. It is traditionally the weapon of the sea gods, especially Poseidon or Neptune. In the story of Poseidon, the Cyclops and the king of the sea forged the trident and then used it to strike a rock to provide water for the Acropolis in Athens. In Roman mythology, Neptune uses the weapon to strike the earth and produce the first mythical horse of war to pull the warrior's chariots in battle.

The trident appears in other mythology, including Indian and Jewish teachings. In Hindu mythology, the goddess Kali and the god Shiva are often pictured with a trident representing three important concepts of the religion.

### Arondight

A famous character in Arthurian legend, Lancelot, was the lover of Queen Guinevere and a famous knight of the round table. His sword was named after the phrase "The unfading light of the lake."

### Ascalon

St. George used the Ascalon sword to slay the dragon. Its name has been used in numerous video games in the creation of magical weapons in fantasy realms.

**Caladgolg**

The Ulster hero Fergus mac Roich wielded this mighty sword to create colorful arcs when he slew his opponents. His followers knew he had been successful when they saw the rainbow-like arcs formed by his sword.

**Dainsleif**

The Norse King Hogni used this weapon to inflict wounds that never heal. It was forged by the dwarves in return for gold and was considered to be one of the deadliest weapons in mythology.

**Excalibur**

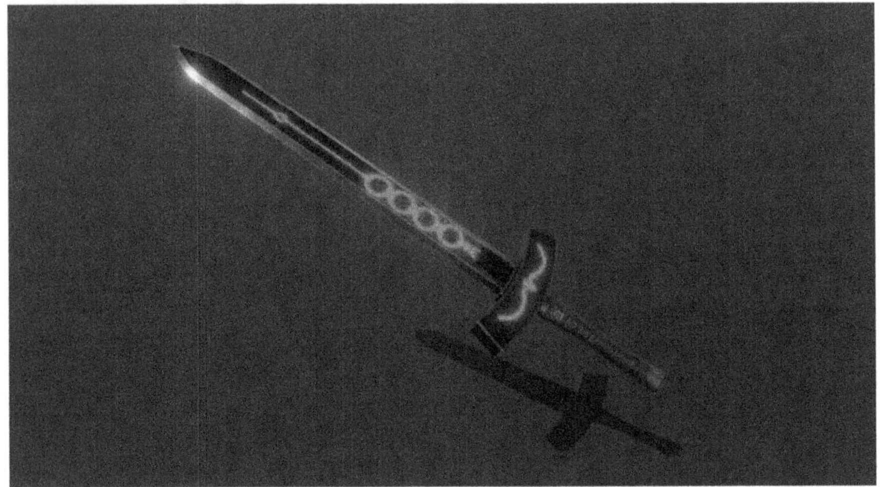

**The Excalibur is thought to be imbued with magical powers.**



The sword of King Arthur was pulled from the stone to determine who should rule England. Different stories have multiple legends regarding the stone, which was thought to be imbued with magical powers.

**Fragarach**

The magical sword of Nuada is a famous figure in Irish mythology. It was forged by the ancient Celtic gods and could inflict wounds that would never heal and also command the weather. It could also force the opponent to speak the truth when the blade was held against its opponent's throat.

## Gambanteinn

A legendary wand-like dagger that appears twice in the Poetic Edda in Norse mythology. It was given as a gift to Harbaror when he outwitted a giant in one poem. In another poem, the dagger was used by Skirnir to threaten the giantess Gerd with her father's death if she refused to stop her wandering and stay away from the human realm.

## Gram

The sword of Sigurd was used by the legendary Germanic hero of Norse mythology. He drew the sword from a tree trunk at a feast where a stranger had placed it. Unknown to the revelers, the stranger was Odin in disguise, and the sword was Gram. Everybody tried but failed until it came to Sigmund, who drew the sword with ease. Everybody coveted the sword, and Sigmund fought many battles to keep it safe. During one battle, Odin split the sword into two pieces, and Sigmund's wife took the parts and hid them.

When Sigmund died, a dwarf named Regin came to teach his son Sigurd the ancient arts and how to battle the dragon Fafnir and claim the treasure it guarded. He helped Sigurd forge the two halves of the Gram sword together to use as a weapon against the dragon. He eventually killed Fenrir with a single blow to the left side. Because the victory was so impressive, the sword was burned alongside the body of Sigurd, and it was never mentioned in mythology after the funeral pyre was lit.

## Hovod

The mythical sword of the guardian of the Bifrost. It was made from Heimdallr and was reputed to choose by whom it was owned. It represents the blessings and strengths of the gods and would also incorporate the personality of the user. It is referred to as the key to the Bifrost Bridge that joins the nine realms and the human world.

## Laevatein

Some Norse believers consider this to be an actual sword, while others think it is the mistletoe projectile used to kill the golden god Baldr after Loki, the trickster god, tricked his mother into revealing his weakness.

## Legbiter

The legendary sword of Magnus III of Norway. When the Men of Ulster killed him, his sword was sent home to his wife to signal his death.

**Mistilteinn**

The legendary sword of Hromundr Grippson in Icelandic mythology. He defeated the draugr, the Norse version of the walking dead, who owned the sword and went on to kill over four hundred men with it. The sword was once lost in the water following a magical spell but was later retrieved from a pike's stomach.

**Naegling**

A legendary sharp and gleaming sword from the poem of Beowulf from the Viking era. It is an unusual tale of a hero and his fight with an evil dragon where the sword broke, not because of the strength of the opponent but because of the strength of the hero.

**Ridill**

Another dwarf-crafted sword in Norse mythology is famous as the weapon that cut out the heart of the defeated dragon Fafnir to roast for the victorious Sigurd and his men.

**Skofnung**

A formidable sword with magical powers that was the weapon of the Danish king Holf Kraki. It was said to contain the spirits of the twelve best warriors of the age who had been killed in battle in its mighty shaft. The sword could inflict wounds that could not be healed, but it could also heal wounds that had been sustained in battle. It should never be drawn in direct sunlight and never in the presence of a woman. Is this a misogynist sword, or does it reflect the feeling that women should not be present on the battlefield?

The sword survived its original owner by over five hundred years and featured in tales until it was buried with its owner in 1073. The sword was a well-traveled weapon and even made a pilgrimage to Rome.

**Tyrfing**

Another magical Norse sword was first mentioned in the Poetic Edda and featured in a tale when Odin's grandsons captured two dwarves and forced them to make him a magical sword. It had a golden hilt, would never rust and could pierce stone and metal just as easily as cloth. The dwarves forged the sword but cursed it by declaring it would kill a man every time it was drawn and would eventually kill the owners.

Of course, these swords are mainly mythological, and some historical weapons feature magic and trolldom. If you get the chance to see these magnificent weapons, you should take it; a peek back in history will help you become inspired in your work.

# Historical Swords

## British Ceremonial Swords

Five swords are kept in the Tower of London, including the Sword of Stae, the Curtana, the Sword of Justice, the Sword of Temporality, and the Sword of Mercy. They are magnificent coronation swords with inset jewels and are made of solid gold. Their crimson straps are made of velvet with embroidery in gold.

## Joyeuse

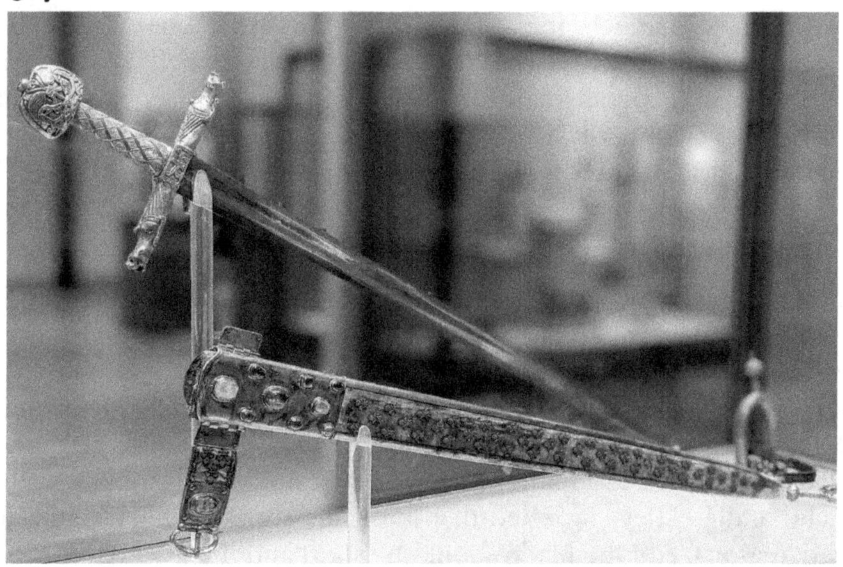

**Joyeuse is Charlemagne's sword.**

*Louvre Museum, CC0, via Wikimedia Commons:*
*https://commons.wikimedia.org/wiki/File:%C3%89p%C3%A9e_du_sacre_des_rois_de_France,_dite_Joyeuse_-_Mus%C3%A9e_du_Louvre_Objets_d%27art_MS_84.jpg*

The sword of the leader Charlemagne who was the first Holy Roman Emperor. It was moved to the Louvre following the French Revolution and has been used in French Coronation ceremonies ever since.

**Lobera**

The name means "wolf slayer," and it was the sword of the King of Castile in 1217. It was a sword of virtue and was bequeathed to his grandson on his deathbed.

**The Sword of Essen**

Given to the area of Essen to commemorate the sainthood of their warriors Cosmos and Damian. It can be seen at Essen Abbey in Germany.

This list of swords and daggers is far from inclusive, as weapons were a major part of mythology. The battle they fought and the victories and losses defined them and made them the legends of their mythology. Today magic has changed, and you need to use your strengths and powers instead of actual weapons.

Decorative daggers and knives can be used to decorate your altar and serve as channels for your energy and force. The athame is a Wiccan tool that can be used in your rituals and spells and can be bought from witchcraft outlets, or you can make your own. It should never be used for actual cutting as it is more powerful when used as a casting tool to direct energy.

## History of the Athame

The first mention of the athame was in 1954 in a book published by Gerald Gardner, where he classed it as the witch's knife. He didn't describe the materials used or the exact use or size but just classed it as a magic weapon. In the 1980s, a more detailed description appeared in a book called the Spiral Dance. This book contained details of the perfect athame, described as a double-sided blade with a black handle. They suggested that the blade should be kept blunt for safety reasons, and the blade should be short and manageable.

In today's practice, the athame is used more like a wand and can be made from traditional steel or even wood. Marble athames and wands look impressive and make your altar look decorative and special. You can use many alternative objects as your athames, like a letter opener and a clay modeling tool. Decorate the handle and make your magic tool more personal.

## Magical Staff

If you like the idea of a magical channel for your energy, you can replace your athame or wand with a staff. It is associated with authority and can make your magic more powerful. Like the wand, it is a powerful male symbol of energy and represents air and fire in elemental magic. Homemade staffs are far more effective than shop-bought staffs and are relatively simple to make.

### Choose Your Wood

First, never cut a live piece of wood from a tree just because you like the look of the branch. Take a walk around a forest and look on the floor for a piece that has already fallen. The length should be between your shoulder height and the ground so you can wield it comfortably. The diameter should be around two inches so you can hold it firmly without breaking it.

You may like to choose the wood depending on its magical properties. Celtic magic has a dedicated Tree Calendar that the Druids created to explain the magical properties of trees.

## The Tree Calendar

### Dec 24th to Jan 20th, the Birch Moon

Birch represents rebirth; the birch is the first tree to regrow if a forest burns down. Birch protects and keeps the user safe and works with birch wands and staff to provide extra energy to spells.

### Jan 21st to Feb 17th Is the Rowan Moon

Associated with Brigid, the goddess of the hearth and home, Rowan wood is also associated with self-improvement and travel. It is a powerful wood to encourage lost spirits' souls to move on and leave the astral plane.

### Feb 18th to March 17th Is the Ash Moon

Yggdrasil, the mystical tree of life in Norse tales, was an ash tree. The wood can be used to encourage inner journeys and astral traveling. It protects you from the spirits that may harm you and all forms of negative energy. Use the ash wood to induce prophetic dreams to tell you what lies ahead for you in both professional and personal matters.

### March 18th to April 14th Is the Alder Moon

Alder wood is often found by riverbeds and is believed to form the bridge between the heavens and earth. It connects the user to the faerie world and encourages them to help your work become more successful. Alder wood is used to make whistles to summon the air spirits and can be made into magical musical instruments.

### April 15th to May 12th Is the Willow Moon

The willow is a tree of mystery and protection. It is often found near cemeteries to protect the dead, and the wood can bring protection to your spells. Use willow wood to encourage healing and growth.

### May 13th to June 9th Is the Hawthorn Moon

Hawthorn wood is steeped in male potency, and its wood can be used to promote fertility and conception. The wood has a potent phallic feel and can be a powerful way to attract passion and love.

### June 10th to July 7th Is the Oak Moon

The mighty oak towers over the other trees in the forest and is a sacred tree to Druid magic. Use the wood to fashion a staff to give protection and promote success and financial luck. It helps to cast a spell for success in business and work situations.

### July 8th to August 4th Is the Holly Moon

The evergreen Holly tree symbolizes immortality and the circle of nature. Use it to bring good luck and safety to your magic and bring a sense of communing with nature to your work.

### Aug 5th to Sept 1st Is the Hazel Moon

Hazel switches are especially effective for dowsing and divination purposes. The wood is related to wisdom and knowledge and can be used to re-inspire artistic and creative projects. Use hazel to get your muse back and become involved with your dreams.

### Sept 2nd to Sept 29th Is the Vine Moon

As we know, wine was a popular drink of the Norse gods and commoners. The wine is brewed from grapes that come from vines, so it is no surprise that the vine symbolizes both happiness and anger. When wine is imbibed, some people become euphoric while others grow wrathful and show their rage. Use the wood to span these emotions and add balance to your work. You must include dark and light aspects to get the most powerful magic in your life.

**Sept 30th to Oct 27th Is the Ivy Moon**

Ivy is a hardy plant that can exist even when the host plant has died, and the wood from ivy is the perfect way to celebrate the cycle of life and death. Use it to improve your love spells and remove toxicity from your life.

**Oct 28th to Nov 23rd Is the Reed Moon**

Not strictly a tree, but reeds are used to attract the souls of the dead. They are made into haunting instruments that can help you collaborate with spirits and conduct successful séances. Use a reed staff to celebrate your ancestors and ask for their wisdom in your work.

**Nov 24th to Dec 23rd Is the Elder Moon**

Elder wood is used to protect against demons and other negative energies. It helps you to rejuvenate yourself and your spirit.

While traditional daggers and swords are only used for decorations, you can still wield some powerful weapons in your magic. Use the knowledge of wood to forge impressive wands and staff to add potency and direction to your work.

# Chapter 6: The Usage of Cord Magic

Witchcraft involves tools and magical objects that can be decorative or sacred but can also involve everyday objects. What do you think of when you say the word cord? Surely the most important cord of all is the umbilical cord. This is the magical piece of skin that keeps every baby healthy. It feeds the fetus, supplies it with oxygenated blood, and is still attached after birth. Cutting the umbilical cord is an important part of the birth process. The remnants of the baby's belly button cord stay with them throughout their lives as an important reminder of their ultimate connection with the woman who gave birth to them.

**Cord magic is a powerful source.**

*https://unsplash.com/photos/0ujNS9PMFhM*

When you use electrical instruments, the chord is the power source, and when we put on shoes, a cord is often used to make them secure. Cords are an intrinsic part of some of our most important instruments, and we have vocal cords to make our voices resonate. Cords are flexible and can be manipulated to suit our needs, making them an especially useful tool in magic. Cords bind and keep separate elements together, making them important in spell work.

## The History of Cord Magic

Once again, we look to Gerald Gardner and his revival of the Wiccan practice in the 1950s in England. He refers to the Cingulim or the witch's cord which represents the basic measurements of the witch's body or a standard length of nine inches. Nine is an important number in magic, but the cords relating to individual magic are especially potent. Cords are issued to witches who are classed as teachers, and they remain the property of the coven until the witch dies or leaves the coven for personal reasons.

In religion, cords are part of rituals that concentrate on meditation or prayers. Catholicism involves a cord of beads known as the rosary that helps the person praying to count their blessings and concentrate on their devotions. In Buddhism, the Lama will bless cords for the wearer to bring luck and bless them with Buddha's spirit. They would be worn around the wrist until they wore out and fell off. The cords' colors would signify the blessing's meaning and make them more effective.

Cords can be used individually or together to form magical effects. They can be combined with knot magic to do spells for all areas of magic and to complete goals in all areas of your life. In the following sections, we will explore some of the more powerful ways to use knots and cords in magic. First, we will find out how to use color to add intention to your work and what the assorted colors mean in cord magic.

## Colors of the Cords

If your spells are all-purpose, then use neutral tones and avoid color. White cords are easily available and can represent the beginning of a new era and the purity of new beginnings. Gray and white cords will help you practice your new skills without worrying about your magic being misinterpreted, but when you are ready to add color, use this chart to give focus and intention to your spell.

**Black:** Wisdom, casting out, banishing, protection, self-examination, dream work, and astral communication.

**Blue:** The color of the element water, cleansing, happiness, devotion, forgiveness, and calm.

**Brown:** The earth element, making dreams happen, building relationships, forming roots, making financial decisions, and connecting with nature.

**Gold:** Monetary success, masculinity, justice, good health, the power of persuasion, solar magic, God connections, sacred energy, and the power of plenty.

**Green:** Money and financial success, natural magic, working with herbs, creativity, growth, and physical success.

**Indigo:** The spiritual world, the Crown chakra, psychic development, prophecy, self-realization, and connecting with the Divine self.

**Lavender:** Calmness, peace of mind, higher understanding, and learning.

**Orange:** Harvesting ideas and knowledge, motivation, energy, self-exploration, mental strength, hope, forward-thinking, creativity, and the power to adapt.

**Pink:** Self-love, new relationships, romance, forgiveness, friendship, and developing a more caring attitude.

**Purple:** Global issues, inclusivity, leadership, mystery, wisdom, luck, and liberation.

**Red:** The fire element, cleansing, new beginnings, sexual success, fertility, vitality, positive energy, and passion.

**Silver:** The feminine energy of the moon, connecting with the earth and her feminine energy, interpreting dreams and astral traveling.

**Yellow:** The air element, happiness, solar energy, increased focus, trust, self-confidence, new goals, improved memory, and inspiration.

## Numerology in Cord Magic

If you incorporate cord magic with knot magic, you'll use numerology to make your spells more focused. The number of knots you use helps you add symbolism and intent to your work and make your results more impressive. Various numerology interpretations depend on cultural influences, but this simple reference list will help you get started. As you become more experienced, you can change the representation of the numbers to suit your subjective experiences. For instance, your birth date or lucky number may become an important part of your equation.

**One:** The higher being, the masculine energy, and the ultimate symbol of your willpower and your ability to influence your world.

**Two:** The sacred partnership and feminine energy, the power of duality and reconciliation, kindness, and sensuality.

**Three:** Youth, casting off adult worries, the power of play, action, happiness, humor, forward-thinking, and dreams.

**Four:** Laying foundations, responsibility, being part of a team, ethics, morality, financial stability, and caution.

**Five:** Opportunities, new projects, adventure, the strength of courage, frivolity, global inclusion, and awareness.

**Six:** Healing, mending relationships, true love, binding, support, and the power of teamwork.

**Seven:** Spirituality, heightened perception, knowledge, wisdom, the strength to survive, clear thinking, forward-looking, and optimism.

**Eight:** Responsibility, judgment, seeking power, authority, and leading from the front.

**Nine:** Humanity, benevolence, charity, responsibility, and awareness.

These nine numbers combine to form multiple numbers in magic and can be described by a simple incantation that witches and magic practitioners have adopted for hundreds of years.

## Knot Incantation

*"By the knot of just one, the magic has been spun,*
*By the knot known by two, the meaning is true,*
*By the knot we call four, the spell is deemed pure*
*By the knot of the five, the spell comes alive,*
*By the knot called six, the magic is fixed,*

*By the knot numbered seven, the word is sent to the heavens,*

*By the knot I call eight, I have sealed my spells fate,*

*By the knot we call nine, all magic shall be mine."*

## Materials You Can Use for Cord Magic

Your basic materials set the intention for your spells. Here are some suggestions for the use of more diverse materials to make your spell personal:

- **Chains:** thin metal chains from jewelry can center your intentions if your spell is for someone else or yourself by using treasured chains from your jewelry box or heirlooms.
- **Floss:** Dental floss is a colorful and inexpensive way to use alternative cordage.
- **Laces:** Shoelaces, laces from corsets, or other clothing will make the spell concentrate on the owner.
- **Leather:** Supple strips of colored leather make your work more durable and long-lasting.
- **Ribbon:** The choice is immense, with ribbons of all widths, lengths, and colors available from local sources.
- **Thread:** Cotton threads are easy to use but can be delicate.
- **Twine:** Colorful and durable.
- **Wire:** Craft wire is a straightforward way to use metal forms of cord to provide a hardwearing way to create knots.

If you do choose fabrics, stay away from synthetic materials. They will be less effective than natural materials, absorbing the magical intentions more thoroughly and retaining their energy. Use wool, silk, or other natural ingredients rather than nylon or other synthetic materials.

## The Intentions behind Cord Magic

Cord magic is a strong way to bind energies together, and when you use certain colors and numerology combined to direct the magical energies. It can be used for all applications and uses and is one of the most versatile types of magic available.

## Protection Spell

Use the cords to bring negative energy to your work and keep it wrapped in your finished cord work. Use red, white, silver, or black cords and the numbers six and eight. Anoint your cords with the essential oil you feel protected by, sage and pine perhaps, and use pine needles to provide a base to work on.

Take the cords and weave them together to form a rope while you recite the following:

*"These cords are my purity, and they will keep me safe from darkness. Make them strong and pure to keep me from the energy they keep secure."*

Now imagine all the negativity in your life becoming trapped by the cords and disappearing from your life. Now imagine a blinding white light bathing your work area in purity. Once the rope has been formed, secure the ends tightly and place it where you feel safe. Take it with you when you leave the house or leave it in place to guard your space.

## Binding Spell

If you are troubled by a certain person or situation, you can create a powerful cord to break the connections that bring you strife.

Take a cord that feels personal to you and represents your energy or use a combination of colors and materials; the choice is yours.

Make a knot in the cord and say, *"I cast you from my life* (insert name or situation) *my joy you will no longer steal."*

This is your binding knot and should stay knotted no matter what.

The second knot should happen underneath the first and is done as you say, *"I banish you (insert name) from my earthly life, freeing myself from all of your strife."*

The third knot should then be tied, saying, *"I cast you out (name) on this knot number three; your power will nevermore affect me."*

The fourth knot should be tied, saying, *"I expel you (name) from my memory and dreams and pray this charm will keep me safe."*

Keep the cord in a safe space and anoint it with your oils or crystals. If you feel any negativity returning, undo the first three knots and repeat the process. Never undo the binding knot, as you will release the negativity which may have increased.

## Cooperation

If you struggle with other people being difficult and crave more balance and harmony in your life, trust simple cord magic. Choose several cords to represent the people causing you difficulties and name them. Make the cords form a braid as you concentrate on the people and situations they represent.

Say this incantation as you work: *"I call on the universe to create harmony between these elements, help us bring together our individual strengths and skills to form a team. I thank the powers that be for their cooperation and love."*

## Creating Strong Ties

When you want something to happen, you should use cord magic to encourage it to happen. For instance, if you are applying for a job, create a cord union between yourself and the position you want.

Take a cord to represent yourself and one for the job. Weave them together as you say the phrase, *"I want this job, and I deserve it, let magic help me show my true self and how I fit the position."* Remember, if you get the job and then leave, don't forget to undo the knot.

## Love and Marriage

Pagans and Wiccan ceremonies often include handfasting and ribbons to bind couples. Trolldom embraces all pagan rites and encourages using brightly colored ribbons and cords to signify the union. For friendship purposes, make simple colored bracelets to give to your friend to signify your connection. Using colors and patterns to show love is a decorative way to signify affection.

## Good Luck Cords

The options are innumerable for making a lucky charm cord. Use your knowledge of the significance of colors and numbers to create a lucky cord. Use green cords for money and pink for love, and add beads or stones to create a decorative item for your altar. The sky is the limit; you can create as many as you like.

Use cords to add magic to physical objects. For example, when job hunting, take the business card of any companies you want to work with and add your resume to the bundle. Wrap the cord of your choice around the papers and say the following, "*Luck and prosperity be mine, make these people see me shine.*" Now store the cord and bundle in a safe place and contact the companies. Then just wait for the interviews to start rolling in.

## Self-Improvement

Create decorative cords to represent the areas of your life that need improvement. If your love life is hectic, use red or pink. If your finances are suffering, use green. Tie the separate cords around your wrist and use them to focus when you are dealing with your issues. Just touching the relevant cord will bring your focus to the forefront and energize you.

## Weather Magic

Witchery based on weather has been used for generations. In Norse times the weather influenced every part of life, and it was important to influence it in any way possible. Sailors would create a strong cord with three knots to indicate the strength of the required winds. One knot represents a breeze, two represent a sailing wind, and three for a gale. Farmers would use a similar method to represent rain; one knot is a shower, two a steady rain, and three a full-on downpour.

However you use them, knots and cords are a simple and available way to practice magic. Beginners can experiment with their materials and create colorful and decorative magical pieces to wear or display in their sacred spaces. Having fun is an intrinsic part of the magic process, and cord magic is lots of fun.

# Chapter 7: Unlocking Elf Magic

Elves play an important role in Norse mythology and are a race of beings who seem to encapsulate the beautiful features of humans but who can quickly turn and become wrathful. They seem to be perfect and live a magical life dancing in the woods and frolicking with the creatures that live there, but on closer examination, they merely reflect what we expect from perfect beings. Once you step into their realm, you incur their wrath and will soon fall ill or begin to develop symptoms of a disease. No matter how you apologize and try to retreat, it doesn't work. You have been elf-shot, and the repercussions are severe and sometimes deadly.

**Elves play an important role in Norse mythology.**

https://pixabay.com/es/illustrations/cl%c3%a1sico-arthur-rackham-victoriano-1722318/

## Elves in Mythology

Tales from Denmark, Scandinavia, and other Nordic areas are filled with elven references. They are described as fair creatures who are luminous in their appearance and seem to remain youthful for hundreds of years. If they do age, it is at a slow rate unperceivable to human eyes, and they are often referred to as "the white people." They are mercurial characters who appear to be friendly to their human cohorts but are quick to anger if they believe they are under threat. Their punishments include illness, night terrors, physical attacks, and cruel pranks played on their victims. However, when humans feel ill with natural diseases, they often turn to elves to help cure them.

European mythology contained stories of elven birth and the need for human midwives and wet nurses. It is believed that when an elf gives birth, the only way the child will survive is with human help. The elves would choose a skilled midwife who would often be married to a preacher to return to the elven world with them, accompanied by a series of wet nurses who had recently given birth to their own children.

This group of women would stay in the elven realm until the child was deemed healthy enough to survive without their help. This raised concerns for women who could potentially be called upon to fulfill the role because if they ate or drank any food in the elven world, they would be prevented from returning to Earth. Any hospitality given and received meant they would be banished to spend the rest of their lives among the elves. It is unclear if the women were given any choice about their journey, but there are numerous tales of women keeping packed food and water just in case they were called to attend an elf birth.

## The Story of Peter Rahm

A preacher named Peter Rahm was married to a midwife, which was a common pairing at the time. Mystical elves summoned her to attend their child's birth and help them deliver the baby. She agreed and traveled to the elven realm, where she performed her duties. When she was there, the grateful parents offered her food and drink, which she gracefully refused. They offered her a bed to rest in and water to wash with, both of which she refused. Once her duties were completed, she returned to the Rahm household. The following day the couple found a bag containing pieces of silver, a gift from the elves for her ministrations.

## A Cautionary Tale of the Midwife and the Elf

A Danish tale tells of an elf visiting Earth on Christmas Eve to seek the help of a midwife to attend the birth of his child. The birth was successful, and the midwife stayed with the elf wife while the husband took the newborn child away to trick a newlywed human couple into giving away their fortune for his child. While her husband was away, the wife told the midwife to refuse any hospitality she was offered while she was in the elven realm. She explained that she had been a mortal woman who had worked as a midwife but made the error of accepting food while attending the birth. Because of this, she could not return to her human realm and was cursed to spend the rest of her life with the elves. The midwife followed her instructions and could return to Earth once the husband returned.

## Elves and Relationships with Humans

As with most Norse tales, relationships often span diverse groups of beings and lead to offspring. Odin, Loki, and other deities often dabbled with other beings to produce some of the most memorable children in mythology. Sex, love, and passion are the driving forces in most of the Norse tales, so mating with creatures who are so beautiful is inevitable. Some tales tell of elves seducing unwitting humans into having sex with them, while others tell of love stories and consensual pairings. The children from these unions are often incredibly attractive and go on to do remarkable things.

These half-human and half-elven children appear to live human lives and are often destined to be great healers and well-versed in magical powers. They appear to be benevolent creatures who are both beautiful inside and out. In ballads and tales of these unions, the human partner will often have to fulfill a task to win the hand of their elf bride. One popular task was to visit the elf realm and rescue a human who had been trapped there to win their spouse's hand in marriage.

## Wayland the Smith

Perhaps the most famous elf in Norse mythology is Wayland the smith, known as Volund in the ancient texts. He appeared in a Scandinavian tale around the ninth century BC when he was featured in a story about king Nithuth and his terrible fate.

The elf and his brother take wives who are part of the Valkyries who stay with them for a couple of years but then fly away. The brother sets off on a mission to find them while Wayland stays home and forges a series of rings enhanced with gems to present to his wife when she returns. King Nithuth hears of his labor and visits the elf's home as he sleeps. The king took the most beautiful ring and left. When the elf awoke, he thought his wife had returned, only to discover the ring had been stolen. He visits the king's palace and reclaims his treasure.

The king then accuses the elf of theft and gives his sword and treasures to his wife and daughter. He cuts the elf's hamstrings and banishes him to a deserted island with instructions to craft precious objects for the king for the rest of his life. Nithuth's sons visit the island to see the objects the elf has created and are killed by the vengeful elf, who then makes cups from their skulls and gems from their eyes while he fashions a brooch from their teeth. The king's daughter visits Wayland to ask him to mend her ring, the one he originally made for his wife. The pair drink together, and the princess falls asleep in the chair. Wayland then makes her his lover, and she is bound to him when she falls pregnant.

There is a gap in the story, but it seems that king Nithuth then summons the crafty elf to explain what happened to his sons and his daughter. Wayland makes the king swear no harm will come to him or his pregnant wife, the princess, before he confesses to killing the two princes. The king agrees, and the story concludes with the elf and his bride flying away and staying safe.

## The Tale of Tam Lin

Although it originated in Scotland, the tale of Tam Lin travels well through Europe. It is based on the elf Tam Lin being captured by the queen of the fairies and eventually being rescued by a mortal girl. Tam is a crafty elf who claims the virginity of any maiden who passes through his forest, which includes a young maid called Janet. She returns home, finds out she is pregnant – and challenges the elf about her condition.

She is determined to keep the baby but is forced to take a herb that will induce her to miscarry. She returns to the forest where Tam Lin lives to find the herb and questions the elf about his origins. He tells her he was once a mortal man who fell from his horse, was captured by the fairy queen, and held against his will. He tells her he is scheduled to become a sacrifice to the gods of hell on Halloween, and they devise a plan to rescue him.

Tam tells Janet he will be riding a white horse, and she must pull him off the horse and catch him to rescue him from his deadly fate. He warns her the fairies will turn him into all manner of beasts to force her to drop him, but he won't harm her. The night of Halloween arrives, and Janet waits in the forest for the elven parade. She spots Tam on his white horse and pulls him from the saddle. When she catches him, the fairies turn him into a series of beasts, but she still keeps hold of him. They turn Tam into a red-hot piece of coal, and she is forced to cast him into the well.

She hides him from the fairies when he emerges as a naked human man. The queen is angry but agrees that Janet has fulfilled her task and lets Tam return to his mortal form. The pair leave the forest together and live happily ever after.

## Isabel and the Elf Knight

Of course, this is mythology; not all tales are filled with love and happiness. The elfin knight was a handsome elf with beatific features and a seemingly kind demeanor. He blew into his horn and declared his love for Lady Isabel, whose heart is won over. She agrees to travel with him to the greenwood to marry him and have his children.

It all changed when the pair arrived at the wood, and the elf knight showed his true colors. He told Isabel he had already killed seven princesses to amass his fortune, and he was planning to kill her to steal her treasures and make her his eighth victim. However, Lady Isabel is a smart cookie and tells the elf she realizes she has been beaten. She tells the elf to rest his head on her knee and spend some time together before she meets her fate. He does so, and she lulls him to sleep with a song, binds him with his own belt, and then kills him with a knife.

## Elf Folklore

There have been many representations of elves and their powers in the past, but they differ in certain cultures and mythology. They are mystical creatures who can cause illness and cure them. They are linked to changelings by stories of elves who favored human babies over their own, especially ones born to parents with fair features. The tale suggests that the tithe to hell that had to be paid every seven years meant they could sacrifice a changeling rather than one of their own.

When the elves stole a human baby, it was believed they left an elf baby behind, which was then identified as a changeling. The infant may appear to be human, but they had strange afflictions that identified them as changelings. The most recognizable symptom was their need to eat more than human babies, which signaled a serious dilemma for the parents. They often chose to kill the baby before it could develop into a child to ensure the changeling caused them no harm.

This may seem chilling to us today. Babies were killed for being different, but back then, there were no other explanations for children being unusual. People believed that supernatural forces ruled their lives and blamed them for any abnormalities.

Norwegian folklore tells of the spirits of the dead returning in elf form. The tale of Olaf the Holy sees his ancestors returning to the grave of Norway's first saint to find an elf residing there. They believe it is the spirit of the old king and erect a signpost at the burial ground reading "Olaf the elf of Geirstad."

Elves' true magic seemed to explain strange events like the birth of a baby with deformities or illnesses that seemingly had no origin. They were blamed for the most unusual events, and the prefix elf was attached to even mundane problems to explain why they happened. For instance, if a person's hair became knotted or tangled around a random object, it was called an elf-knot.

Today we have more scientific and modern explanations for unusual events and do not need to explain them away with supernatural reasoning, but that shouldn't stop us from being interested in elves. In Iceland, they believe so strongly in elves and their underground realm that in 2012 a law was passed to stop construction on a road that would pass through an area believed to be the habitat of elves. The protest was taken to the highest courtroom and led to an enforced law forbidding any interference in areas believed to be inhabited or of significance to elves anywhere in Iceland.

We still believe in elves at Christmas and picture the little green men and ladies helping Santa at the North Pole make presents for the world's children. Who can forget the portrayal of Will Ferrel playing Buddy the elf in the classic movie Elf? It is far removed from the Nordic version of the beautiful creatures described in their mythology but still relevant. Elves' magic seems to be their trickery, playfulness, and belief in themselves. Surely, the best way to adopt your elf magic is to be industrious, seek the best for yourself, and keep faith in whatever you believe in.

# Chapter 8: Dwarf Magic

Dwarves are practical creatures, and although they live in a world of magic and witchcraft, they only believe in practical magic. They dismiss all other forms of magic as sorcery and forbid themselves and other dwarves from practicing it. Although they have links with the elves, there is a bitter dispute over their use of healing magic and potions. Dwarves only trust magic they have control over and magic that produces things. They despise the sea and heavens and would never live anywhere other than areas with healthy resources they can utilize in their work.

Dwarves don't use the term magic but attach the practice to their preferred term of crafting. In this way, dwarves practice craft magic and produce the most amazing objects in mythology. Theirs is a magic of things, and they have their own way of making seemingly everyday materials into magical and wondrous objects. Some Norse believers see elves as magical beings, gnomes are master craftsmen, but dwarves exceed them in their knowledge and skills. They are short, squat creatures with misshapen and ugly features, but their minds are filled with mysteries and wonder. They knew Newton's laws way before Newton and intrinsically understood the laws of dynamics and thermodynamics. They used this knowledge to make themselves indispensable to the gods and goddesses who would repeatedly call on them to produce their jewelry, weapons, and other magical objects.

# Worthy Dwarves from Norse and Scandinavian Mythology

There are so many references in Norse mythology that it would take another book to list them all and their importance. The Prose Edda and the Poetic Edda are littered with tales of the dwarves and how they played a significant role in Norse beliefs, but here we can study just a few of them and get an idea of the part they played in society.

Alberich appears in Germanic tales from the medieval poems known as the Thidriksaga, where he is described as the king of supernatural beings.

Austri is one of the four dwarves tasked with holding the skull of Ymir aloft to form the heavens.

Billingr was the father of a young girl who was the object of Odin's lust. He told the god to return that night and claim his prize, but when Odin returned, he found the path blocked by hounds and warriors. Undeterred, Odin returned the next morning to find a female dog tied to the maiden's bed. The lowly dwarf had outwitted the mighty Odin and saved his daughter from her fate.

Durim is the second dwarf ever created and the leader of the powerful group of dwarves known as the monsignor.

Fjalar was one of a pair of dwarves who slew Kvasir and converted his blood into the liquid that formed mead which has inspired scholars and poets ever since.

Galar was the other dwarf who helped Fjalar kill Kvasir.

Ivaldi belongs to a group of skillful dwarves who fashioned vessels for the gods and goddesses. They are acclaimed for their work on the ship the Skipbladnir for Freya and the golden locks they made to replace the hair of Sif when Loki tricked her. They are also the experts behind the sword of Odin.

Mondul was the master behind some of the sturdiest axles, shafts, and handles on the gods' chariots.

Norori supports the northern point of the skull of Ymir that forms the heavens.

Sindri was a dwarf that was so respected Odin used his name as an alternative term for the place where dead souls would gather.

Skirfir is the dwarf of paneling who could create the most sturdy and decorative work from herringbones.

Suori holds the southern point of the skull of Ymir.

Uri was the keeper of the smithy and head of the blacksmiths. He was also known as King of the Slag.

Vestri holds the western point of the skull of Ymir.

This list is far from comprehensive, and the lands where they lived are also referenced throughout Norse teachings. The dwarves are enigmatic and secretive about their skills and prefer to work far from prying eyes. The bulk of their crafting involves simple objects with magical elements, and the forge where they are created is a sacred place.

## The Craft

Although dwarves were mainly involved with mundane work when they were called to "craft" certain items, four individual elements were involved. A specialized forge was formed using algebraic calculations, the character of the crafter, the material used, and the construction methods. All these elements made each forge special and personal to the dwarf who used it. Another noteworthy element of dwarfish crafting is the Kunzler, or the primary dwarf craftsman. He would normally have a Knecht working with them, a Norse version of the apprentice, and the master dwarf was known as the Kunzler.

The tools they used were bequeathed to them by their master or were crafted by their own hands, and the dwarves were very wary of their knowledge being abused by outsiders. They formed their own guilds and only allowed trusted members of the community to join them, and they never wrote their knowledge in books or other texts. The apprenticeship was long and arduous, and only the most gifted dwarves would complete it and become Kunzler's themselves.

## Dwarf Worlds

There is little natural light in the world of the dwarf. They don't see black as a shade, just a state of being. There is darkness in the world that lies under the stone and shade that lies beneath the light. The brightest part of the dwarf world is the flame from their sacred forge. Dwarf hell is a place where they cannot function. It is a world of mute paralysis where the air is dank and cold, and the souls that live there will never feel warmth again.

The dwarf ethos is based on gems, stones, and precious metals, and while humans and gods would refer to the beauty of a gem or precious stone, the dwarf would know the complete history of every piece they use in their craft. Every material has a history that goes deep and includes where it was originally mined, who found it, and how its past has shaped it. A reverence makes the finished items so magical they are highly sought after by all.

This brings us to the final element of the dwarf magic, payment. In all the Norse myths, dwarven magical items cost potential owners a high price which could be money, gold, or debt of favor the dwarf could use to boost their social position.

## Modern Dwarf Magic

Today we see dwarves as fictional creatures that feature in fantasy stories and as underground creatures who do their work in secret and play their part in the tales that feature them. But what if we consider their ethos in more practical forms? Can we perform dwarf magic and become Master of Physical transformation?

Yes, we can. There are so many resources available to learn from that we can emulate the dwarf magic from Norse mythology. Create beautiful and sacred pieces to use in your own form of craft magic and bring the energy of these magical creatures. If dwarves existed today, they are the most likely form of Norse creature that would blend in. They are humanoid and industrious and would contribute to society.

## Study Gemstones and Crystals to Use in Your Magic

Nature's magic is all around you, and knowing the properties of certain items will boost your spells and rituals. Build an impressive collection that will be useful and beautiful.

### Agate

A brown or gold stone agate is used to boost magic related to mental issues like discovery, healing, and overcoming mental health issues. It will bring you energy and help you overcome any loneliness or sadness you may be experiencing. Carry it with you to bring energy to your day, or place it under your pillow to make your sleep more restful and freer from bad energy.

### Amethyst

A colorful purple crystal amethyst is connected to the element of water and is used to sharpen the mind. Use it to cleanse your sacred areas and create a light and sacred space. Ancient Greek practitioners used the crystal to avoid inebriation, so carry it in your pocket if you are on a night out to avoid any possible drunkenness.

### Bloodstone

A green stone with specks of red and gold, this powerful stone will bring solar energy and connect you to the planet Mars. It has deep connections to the blood and is used to soothe blood disorders or to calm menstrual issues. If you are trying to conceive, carry a bloodstone or use it in fertility rituals to improve your chances of falling pregnant.

### Carnelian

**Carnelians are used in grounding spells and rituals.**

*jaja_1985, CC BY 2.0 <https://creativecommons.org/licenses/by/2.0>, via Wikimedia Commons: https://commons.wikimedia.org/wiki/File:Carnelian_-_tumble_polished_stone.jpg*

The red/orange hue of the carnelian streaked with white is comparable to the landscapes found in the American southwest area. It is associated with the element earth and is used in grounding spells and rituals. It is a potent fertility stone and can be sued to treat impotency and infertility. Use carnelian to keep your magic tools free from negative energy and create a talisman from carnelian to use as a magic shield.

**Diamonds**

Tied to both elements of air and fire, they are also linked with solar energy and the heavens. Although they are almost always flawed, they still have powerful energy and can be used to promote astral communications and fortune-telling. It also enhances meditation and is used in rituals to promote Intuition and mental clarity.

**Garnets**

These blood red and sometimes purple have strong connections to the element of fire and the eternal goddess. However, they are a strong female-related gem that can be used in all manner of spells. Use garnets to uncover the mysteries of the female body and deal with any female issues. Be aware that garnets that have been obtained through deception or theft carry a curse that remains until they are returned to their rightful owner. Garnets are especially important in balancing energies and connecting the physical and spiritual parts of the human psyche.

**Iron Rose**

Also known as the hematite, this is one of the most important stones you can have in your collection. It is used in Feng Shui to create safe spaces so you can use it to protect your home and sacred area. Place it on your windowsill and above your door to create a safe environment. Carry iron rose stones with you to encourage psychic communications and drive out stress. It will improve your confidence and make you more decisive and successful.

**Jade**

Used in Eastern magic, jade is a stunning green stone that can appear to be white, gray, or even pink in different lights is a calming stone connected to the element of the earth. Use it to heal internal organs and bring a balanced feeling between your physical and spiritual energies.

### Jasper

This is a robust stone that is brownish-red in color and flecked with other earthy hues. It is associated with the element earth and is used in healing therapies and rituals. It is perfect for grounding yourself and your space after a spell or ritual and can be used to center your energy. Its earthy energy is also associated with sexual potency, and it can help you put the oomph back in your sex life if you place it underneath your mattress.

### Lazurite

Also known as lapis lazuli, this uniquely beautiful stone comes in an array of hues ranging from pale blue to the deepest shade of blue, just like the night sky, depending on where it was mined. The color is significantly reminiscent of the element water and is used to treat depression and relieve anxiety. Use it in your magic to encourage psychic connections and to commune with the Divine. Lapis lazuli is a calming element that will aid your mediation and help you reach altered states of consciousness. In Egyptian traditions, the lazurite was often used in funereal rituals and to decorate the sarcophagus.

### Moonstone

As the name suggests, this stone has strong lunar connections and is intrinsically linked to the female deities that use lunar energy. It is the female energy that helps with menstrual and reproduction issues, and it brings a calm and soothing aura when carried. Use it in ceremonies to celebrate the power of Sol and Mani, the Norse god and goddess of the sun and moon. Carry it with you to help you feel calm and balanced, especially in times of stress.

### Obsidian

Black and shiny, this stone has a certain presence and is used to draw the toxins from the blood and body. Use it by placing it beneath your feet while you perform energy work to draw out any negativity and harmful energy. It is strongly connected to the element fire and should be used in rituals for intuition and scrying.

### Opal

Often described as an unlucky stone, the opal has often been misunderstood. It comes in a range of shades ranging from luminescent and pale to dark blue with green and yellow specks. In certain lights, they look like they are lit from within and are especially stunning in candlelight. It links all four elements, making it an essential part of your magic stone collection. Use it to protect your physical space and heal your psychic energy. It has a powerful absorption quality, drawing in both positive and negative forces, making it a powerful enhancer when used in magic.

### Quartz

There are so many kinds of quartz it is hard to choose which to focus on. Choose rose quartz for romance or white quartz for more general work. The stones are all connected to the four elements and are versatile and powerful when used in healing and protection. They promote spiritual and divine growth and will help you connect to the universe.

### Sapphires

Their regular color is blue, but sapphires also come in white and yellow. They are associated with water and bring the energy that helps you connect to spirit guides and receive their messages.

### Tiger's Eye

The coloring and black banding on this stone gives the impression you are looking into the eye of the tiger, which explains the name. It is connected to the element fire and used for general health spells and rituals. Incorporate it into your life to enhance your self-confidence and protect you from the negative forces of others.

### Turquoise

Associated with Native American practices, this eye-catching stone is blue flecked with black or white. It is a powerful healing stone that brings knowledge and wisdom to whoever wears it.

### Zircon

It looks like a diamond and can be used as a more affordable stone to create the same energy in magic. It has strong sexual energy and is used in rituals for improving relationships and fertility.

# Chapter 9: A Guide to Practicing Trolldom

The practice in this book is designed to help you live better and become the person you want to be. Norse beliefs and trolldom allow you to make choices and be the architect of your own fate. They encourage you to trust your instincts, and this is why there is a significant shift in people choosing to eschew traditional religions in favor of the Nordic ways. They understand that choice and freedom of movement have been restricted for generations and that certain religions focus on fear and punishments as part of their doctrines and seek to rule them with fear and fixed rules.

Why should free-thinking people have to follow archaic rules that have no relevance in modern society? Nordic practices and pagan beliefs put the power back in your hands and give you the freedom to abandon monotheism and embrace a range of deities. Trolldom is a cover-all term for several practices we have covered and a whole lot more. You have no limits to stay within, and every day can be a learning experience. There are multiple resources for you to tap into, and you can get acquainted with like-minded people.

Traditional religions are constantly asking their followers to ask for forgiveness. Maybe their sexuality doesn't conform to the norm. The believers are asked to conform to boring, impoverished archaic rituals that aren't pleasant or fulfilling. Norse and Nordic rituals are filled with passion and beliefs fueled by your desires and needs. You can tailor the magic to work for you and make your life richer in all ways. Doesn't that sound much better than apologizing and asking for forgiveness about things that are beyond your control?

## Nordic Societies

### The Asatru Alliance

This is an American Heathen Group founded in 1994 that offers a safe place for pagans and heathens to meet, share ideas and gain knowledge. Kindreds across the world reach out to each other and practice the ancient Asatru, which predates Christianity and is the main religion that trolldom recognizes.

They offer courses on traditional skills and craftwork from the era and encourage their members to take part. They celebrate the power of mead and its significant role in rituals. They have an online calendar that tells followers what the special holidays are, the date they fall on, and highlights any kindred celebrating these dates.

There are links and resources for people to contact other communities that appeal to them. The Alliance is based in Arizona, but there are communities throughout the world that follow the Nordic ways. The movement began to gain interest in the 1970s and has grown exponentially ever since. It has become the biggest growing religion per capita in the last ten years and especially appeals to younger members of society.

## Why Do the Figureheads in Nordic Beliefs Appeal to Followers?

They are fallible! Simply put, people can relate to them and their lives. Odin, the master of Asgard and the lord of the Norse people, made mistakes. He had affairs, and lower beings tricked him. His love life was complicated, and his children weren't always the best. Freya, Loki, Thor, and Bader are all part of our language thanks to popular culture, but even though the films bear little resemblance to the mythology, they have elevated interest in all things Norse. The whole Norse universe is filled with wonderous beings like the elves and dwarves we have already studied. The gods and goddesses were awe-inspiring and multifaceted. They could be benevolent, fearsome, cruel, or destructive depending on the situation, but they were never boring.

The tales from Norse mythology are filled with death-defying courage, and this is something we can all relate to. As we have already discovered, Nordic religion has no hard and fast rules or doctrines, and trolldom is no different. It suggests that we can all improve and become more productive beings, but it lets us choose how to do that. The virtues that Nordic ways promote are no-brainers; it's just that modern society has caused us to forget the importance of doing the right thing. We are pushed to succeed at any cost, often at the expense of others. When did we get so ruthless that it is okay to trample on people just to become successful or wealthy?

Are fame, wealth, and material needs your driving force? Will you do anything to achieve your goals? Or do you strive to be successful while making the world a better place simultaneously? We can all be ambitious and reach for the stars but let's try to get back to some of the more noble virtues that held fast in the past. Before the advent of technology and industry, before the time when we expected to have everything we wanted with the least effort, there was a code to live by. A series of virtues that meant something to the Nordic people are experiencing a revival as we seek to embrace the values of simpler times.

## The Nine Noble Values of the Viking Folk

Some people may question using Vikings to represent the nobility of the Norse age. Surely, they were bloodthirsty warriors who pillaged monasteries and committed unspeakable acts in foreign lands. That is one view, and, understandably, it is a common conception of the Viking hordes due to media portrayal, but when you study them more closely, there was much more to the Viking race than violence.

They lived in a civilized society that had structure and government. They held courts to decide what was right and how to deal with lawbreakers. Their children were taught noble arts, and both boys and girls were instructed in the art of fighting. They were pioneers who took to the seas to explore and seek new lands for their people, and, most of all, they were farmers. Their knowledge of the land was exemplary, and they had the skill to grow crops in even the bleakest environments. Remember, the Nordic lands are a hostile part of the world with cold and harsh climates and a lack of sunshine that makes even the hardiest crops difficult to cultivate, but the Vikings managed to make these lands fertile, and they thrived.

Vikings lived a warrior lifestyle, but they also embraced wisdom and virtues. They had a noble and true code that coincided with multiple other warrior codes throughout the world. This proves that there was a time when everyone recognized that true character and honor were universal. Following Nordic values may just help us get back to that time.

### Courage

Bravery isn't just needed on the battlefield. It should be something we practice every day. Put your head above the parapet and be heard even when your opinion differs from the mainstream. Stand up for people who don't have a voice and be their champion. Bravery means challenging others and avoiding conforming because it seems like the easier option. Use your wisdom and discretion to choose your battles and avoid acting recklessly, making you look foolish. Be a warrior but fight for things you honestly believe in rather than battles that have already been lost.

### Truth

Honesty seems to be a value that has fallen by the wayside. Lying and untruths are so commonplace they seem acceptable and part of getting what you want. In truth, lying is cowardly and means you can't face the truth. If you know something isn't true or don't believe it to be true, then say so. Don't go along with the lie because it is easier than being honest.

Everyone perceives things differently, and what is true for some may not be for others, and that's okay. The world would be dull if we all thought the same way, but you can be a warrior against lies and still have your own opinions. Live by your truth as far as you can, carry the banner against BS and respect others' rights to believe what they do. You set yourself on a path of lies when you lie to yourself. If you can't be true to yourself, then how can you be true to others?

There is a right way to do things, and, as a warrior, you must choose. The Viking code allowed their warriors to lie back if they were being lied to, challenging their opponents like for like gave them the upper hand. True honor isn't always straightforward; you must decide what is right according to your intentions and do the right thing. Honesty shouldn't be brutal, and discretion is the best part of valor.

### Honor

How many people use the word honor anymore except in wedding vows? There are places of honor that mean they are important and worthy, or there is the quality of knowing what is right. Honors are given to those who do wonderful things, but when it comes to virtues, what we consider honorable matters. Honor is your internal moral compass and not your reputation.

Honor doesn't originate from what other people think of you it is all about what you think of yourself. Noble warriors who live by their moral code will have very few regrets. They have an honorable soul and will have lived ethically and morally sound lives.

### Fidelity

Another seemingly archaic term, fidelity, simply means faithful. Most people associate this virtue solely with marriage, but when you apply it to the rest of your life, you fully understand why it is such an important virtue. Stay true to your friends, your family, and your partner. Viking families believed that if you attacked them, they were under an obligation to fight back. This is different from revenge and means fulfilling an obligation to show fidelity to others. Of course, in modern society, we don't believe in an eye for an eye mentality, and we rely on the law to put right wrongs against us, but that doesn't mean fidelity is a lost virtue.

Show fidelity by entering into a bond with those you hold dear. Let them know you will always be there for them and that you have their back. Never disrespect that bond, no matter what pressures you have to go against them. Be true to your gods, friends, and family; they will see you as a loyal and faithful ally. Take your time making these bonds and only give your fidelity to those who deserve it, as fidelity is a gift that shouldn't be given lightly.

### Discipline

An old Nordic saying tells us, "He who lives without discipline dies without honor," which sums up what happens when we have no self-discipline. This is a tricky virtue as it sometimes means your code of ethics may differ from those that the government or other peers have dictated. Stand fast and be courageous with your choices, you won't perfect self-discipline overnight, and it takes a strength of conviction that will test you. Take control of your emotional responses and exercise self-discipline to gain control of your life.

### Hospitality

Not the most obvious warrior trait, hospitality is nevertheless especially important to the Viking code. They believed that the gods and goddesses regularly visited earth and passed as mortals to evaluate them, and they didn't want to disrespect them should they meet. Viking households welcomed strangers and travelers into their homes and treated them with respect. This virtue is about your personal ethics, regardless of what others deserve. We should always behave to others like we would like them to behave to us.

### Industriousness

Laziness wasn't allowed in Norse times. The land was a cruel mistress and needed to be worked to produce food. The seas were also dangerous to travel and would reward any lack of industry with cruelty and death. True warriors work hard and smart to use their time efficiently. This may seem obvious at work but does your industriousness only apply in the workplace? What about at home? Do you get in from work and expect everything to be done for you? Try becoming more productive in all areas of your life and reap the rewards.

Mediocre is a word that isn't included in Nordic work ethics. They believe that if you are going to do something, you should do it to the best of your abilities. Heighten your expectations, and others will follow. Lead by example and show the world what you are capable of, and your self-respect will grow, and so will your achievements.

### Self-Reliance

Vikings didn't have the welfare state to call on; they believed that their family and friends needed them to survive. They believed that being responsible for your destiny and that of your close circle was down to individuals. When a group of warriors thinks like this, they are individually strong, and when they work as a group, they are invincible.

Too many people rely on others to survive. We seem to have lost that important feeling of self-reliance when you reap benefits stemming from your actions. There is a very selfish side to today's society where we seem to believe we are entitled to certain standards. Of course, how we live is different from the Nordic ways, but that doesn't mean we should expect other people to provide for our basic needs.

Try another way of thinking and be more self-reliant. Save your money for big purchases rather than relying on credit. Be frugal and enjoy the fruits of your labor by considering every cent you spend and appreciating the goods you earn. We all want the best for our families, but are we teaching them the right lessons when we rely on outside sources to provide? No, we aren't, and that needs to stop; bring up your kids to understand that good things come to those who rely on themselves and put in the effort.

**Perseverance**

Have you spotted a common theme in the previous eight virtues? They all need effort and will take time to master, so it seems inevitable that perseverance should apply to all of them and finish the list. There is no point in striving for self-improvement if you don't have the most important virtue: the power to get past obstacles or difficulties and continue, the doggedness to reach your goals or the strength to keep going when the going gets tough. **Perseverance.**

You aren't trying out a warrior's lifestyle for a laugh. Committing to the Nordic trolldom virtues is a lifelong pledge; you either have the qualities it takes, or you don't. No judgment is involved, not all humans are destined to be warriors, but if you have the steeliness of character to fail, get up from that failure, and carry on with the determination to succeed next time, then you are potential warrior material.

## More Modern Ways to Live a Nordic Life

Did you know that in 2016 a report about the happiest places on earth, four of the top five countries were Nordic? Denmark topped the table, and Iceland, Sweden, and Finland came in at three, four, and five. Switzerland was second, and the US came thirteenth. The survey was based on happiness living in their societal structures, the freedom to make choices, the generosity of their compatriots, and their low levels of corruption. They also factored in the social support, GDP per head, and equality levels to calculate a happiness scale.

The US President at the time, Barack Obama, was so impressed with the results he suggested that the Nordic nations should be put in charge of running the world for a while so they could clean things up. So, it is no wonder that people are turning to trolldom, Asatru, and Nordic influences to make their lives better, and here are a few suggestions on how you can embrace the Hygge lifestyle, or what the people in the frozen north describe as the art of living well.

You may not be able to emulate the Nordic countries' equality in education, gender issues, and other societal facilities. Their egalitarian society ensures that every individual has access to the same facilities no matter their heritage. We can, however, Nordify our lives and make them more comfortable, healthy, and content.

### Hygge

Hygge comes from the old Nordic word *hugr*, which means soul, mind, and consciousness. It isn't a fad and isn't all about embracing Scandinavian culture. It is about being in the present and appreciating what is happening around you. It doesn't happen on the Internet, but the global community can add to the experience. Sounds confusing? It isn't but let's explore how being at home with the ones you love is much more important than any other connections.

Another Scandinavian word to learn is *pyt*, which loosely translated means "forget about it" or "okay that happened, so let's move on" and is a breezy, happy way to develop a tricky situation into a positive one. Use it when someone apologizes for something trivial like spilling water on your carpet or catching your arm as you pass. PYT! Move on and get over it! Try it now and experience how good it feels not to sweat the small stuff.

Some people believe the Hygge lifestyle is all about white decorations, candles, huge cushions on a linen sofa, and natural materials decorating the home. It isn't about what you have or don't have; it's about how you live and your human interactions with others. Hygge is all about lack of ostentation and being content with what you have. This doesn't mean that you have no ambition but quite the opposite. Your ambitions are to have a balanced work-play relationship and know how to relax.

### Where to Start

With yourself. Simple as that, take a good look at yourself and what you bring to the table. Are you able to let go of your ego and be yourself with other people? Can you laugh at yourself and be self-effacing? Hygge is about letting your hair down and being part of the moment. Stick your smartphone on hold and look people in the eyes as you toast them with a glass of wine, water, or whatever you have available and see what happens next.

### Scandi Conversations

What are popular topics for Scandi hygge style talks? Anything spontaneous and not concerned with advancement. Don't concentrate on networking (possible the most anti-hygge word ever) or your future; just talk about what matters now. The last film you saw or a funny story about what happened when you went shopping last week. Imagine a Nordic village square filled with locals just chewing the fat about recipes, what is happening with the weather, or local fashions. They are conversations that would have been spontaneous and filled with laughter. Bonding over local issues can be so rewarding, and we have forgotten how to be spontaneous.

Serious conversations can happen, but they don't have to be a matter of life or death. Hygge provides a safe environment where people know they can air their opinions without fear of reprisals. All manner of subjects can be discussed and debated, and that is what Scandi conversations are all about, equality and respect. Why do some people believe happiness is linked to financial status when you look at those who have achieved it and are still unhappy? Scandinavian and trolldom are all about valuing human contact and interaction in their purest form and feeling energized by the company you keep.

## Other Ways to Live Nordic Style

### Get Viking Fit

We all want to get our bodies into shape, and Viking workouts are the perfect way to connect to the Nordic life and get outside more. Check out Scandinavian Fitness online and learn from a former Olympic rower, Linda, how to use crawling exercises, weights, and physical movements outside to get fit. She promises to get you sweaty and out of breath with some amazing results.

### Eat Foods That Are in Season

We are all so used to having all foods no matter the season because we import all goods. Try another way of eating and choose foods and vegetables available to you from local sources. Try foraging and picking wild berries to make your food tastier and healthier. Nordic clean eating is a perfect way to hone your tastebuds to a new type of food cooked from scratch and filled with seasonal favorites.

Add more grains and fish to emulate a Scandi diet, and you will find the food more diverse, affordable, and available. It will help you lower your cholesterol and blood pressure with nutritious ingredients and vitamins. Try the Nordic Cookbook by Magnus Nilsson, who's the head chef at a top Swedish restaurant.

### Get Back to Nature

**Gain a more Nordic understanding by exploring nature.**
*https://pixabay.com/images/id-1072828/*

If you have ever seen any documentaries or programs about the Nordic region, you can't have failed to notice the number of swimming pools, spas, and other outdoor leisure facilities. They don't see inclement weather as a reason to stay in and chill with Netflix. They see it as an opportunity to get out there and experience the joy of the great outdoors. Change your outlook and get in on Nordic by taking more adventurous holidays. No matter where you live, there will be an opportunity for you to take a break in nature. A cabin in the woods or a hiking holiday, it doesn't matter. Get rid of the luxuries and experience the joys of Mother Nature.

**Take a Sauna**

Cleansing should be both internal and external, and Nordic folk love to experience an intense sweat followed by an icy plunge into the water to create the juxtaposition between heat and cold. See if there is a traditional woodfired sauna near you to get those sweat glands working. There is nothing better after a stressful time than to relax in the steam, sweat out the toxins of life, and then immerse yourself in the freezing water.

To summarize, to celebrate trolldom and all things Nordic, you need to create a balance in your life, relationships, food, and emotions. However, you feel you can dip your toe by practicing cord magic and making cute bracelets, or you can go full-on Viking warrior. The choice is yours, and it always will be.

# Bonus Section

A comprehensive guide to the potions from chapter 4 so you can print them and add them to your spell book or book of shadows.

## The Hibiscus Love Potion

This simple herbal tea has no caffeine content and can be consumed both heated and cold. Make a batch to keep in the fridge for when you need a boost of self-confidence.

**What You Need:**

- Hibiscus tea
- Sugar
- Mint leaves
- Pink candle
- Small metal container
- Cup
- Water

Dress your altar with a candle and a white cloth. Turn off all your electronics and keep them out of your sacred area. Play soothing music or just enjoy the silence. Heat the water in the metal container with the candle flame while you recite the following "I am loved, I am worthy of that love, and I accept it with the power of the universe. Bring me a wave of inner peace, and let me rid myself of negativity and darkness while I let the light of the world fill me up."

Add the tea and water to your cup and sweeten to taste. Sprinkle the mint and drink after it has brewed. As you sip the tea, imagine your best life, that job you know you are worthy of, the partner you know you deserve, and see yourself surrounded by the love of people around you.

## A Healing Potion for Low-Level Ailments or to Boost Energy

This is a simple brew that will make you feel energized and drive those nagging ailments away.

**What You Need:**

- 2 small pieces of willow bark
- 1 tbsp. vanilla extract
- 1 tbsp. apple juice
- A pinch of sage
- Pinch of rosemary
- 2 drops of lemon juice
- Water

Dress your altar with a light blue cloth and place the ingredients in your cauldron. Add your preferred base liquid; we have used water in this example and boiled the liquid. As the water boils, recite this mantra "Healing liquid be my balm, stop the pain and heal the harm." Once the liquid has cooled, pour it into a cup and sip the tea while imagining all the pain leaving your body. Imagine the white light filling you with energy and excitement for what the day holds for you, and picture the fatigue leaving your body and floating away into the ether.

## Cold and Flu Potion

**What You Need:**

- Ginger, either dried or ground root
- 1 tbsp. lemon juice
- 1 tbsp. Manuka honey

- A pinch of cinnamon
- Brown sugar
- Water or lemon tea

This can be brewed on your altar or created in your kitchen on the stove. Add all the ingredients to a pot and let it simmer for ten minutes while you recite the following "Magic potion, do your thing, clear my throat so I can sing, let your magic soothe my soul and make me feel forever whole." Once the potion has cooled, sweeten it and drink whenever needed.

## Protection Potion to Keep Negative Energy at Bay

This potion can be ingested to keep you safe or used to sprinkle around your home for added protection. It can be bottled and used for up to three months after it has been brewed.

**What You Need:**

- Jasmin tea bag
- 1 tbsp. Manuka honey
- 2 cloves
- 1 tbsp. lemon juice
- 3 bay leaves
- Sprinkle of black pepper
- Water
- Cup
- Sugar

Dress your altar in gold or red cloth and decorate with your favorite crystals or gemstones. Add anything you feel represents your favorite parts of your life, like your house keys, jewelry, or pictures of your family or friends.

Place the cauldron on the altar, add the ingredients (except the sugar), and repeat the following. "I call on the divine to make me feel safe. Bless me with your all-encompassing energy and shield me from harm. Be my guardian and give me the strength to shield others and myself."

Now take the cauldron to your kitchen and brew the potions. Use it to consecrate your home or drink it depending on your needs. Imagine a bright white dome surrounding all the things you love, and then picture the negative forces being repelled into the dark.

## The Raspberry Honey Potion

This boozy potion is for cleansing and purifying your energy and attracting new love or friends

**What You Need:**

- Raspberry vodka
- Raspberry tea
- Hibiscus tea
- 1 tsp caramel syrup
- Lemon juice
- Honey
- Peppermint cordial
- Ice
- Cocktail shaker or cauldron

You can make the process more magical by dressing your altar in pink, yellow, or white cloths and a couple of candles, but this potion really is just about the end product. Add all the ingredients to your chosen receptacle and either stir or shake. Add the ice as you mix or put it in a glass to cool the liquid. As you sip your potion, thank the gods, goddesses, and the universe for your good fortune and give them cheers for their interest in you and your life.

## Love Potion with Wine

**What You Need:**

- Wine, you can use white or rose
- Fresh peaches
- Raspberries
- Vanilla pods

- Sprig of mint
- Ice
- Glass

Fill a glass with ice and add the wine. As you add the other ingredients, ask the heavens to send you positive energy and a vision of your perfect partner. Once the potion has been stirred and chilled, sip it slowly and imagine how the two of you will look in the future. Thank the goddess of love and romance for her help.

## Sleepy Potion

**What You Need:**

- 1 shot of dark rum
- Cinnamon
- Dark sugar
- Water or milk, depending on your taste
- An orange candle
- Lavender essence
- Cauldron
- Cup

Dress your altar with muted color cloth and place the orange candle on the surface. Put the rum, cinnamon, sugar, and water/milk in your cauldron on the stove and bring it to a boil before letting it simmer for two minutes. Bring the cauldron to the altar, light the candle, and sprinkle the essence on your altar as you pour the potion into a cup. Recite the following "Take me to the land of rest and let my sleep be the best, help me dream of past and present, and show me how to be ready for the future."

Drink the potion and let your eyes droop as you imagine the future filled with love and success.

## Vino for Passion

**What You Need:**

- A bottle of sweet red or white wine
- 5 fresh basil leaves
- 6 red rose petals
- 3 cloves
- 4 apple seeds
- 2 drops of pomegranate essence
- 2 oz. raspberry juice
- A large piece of ginseng root
- Cauldron
- Tea cloth for straining
- Glass jar with a sealable top

Decorate your altar with red and white cloths, and then add white quartz, moonstone, and garnet to the table. Add all the ingredients to the cauldron and take it to the kitchen. Decorate the area you are working in with colored candles and tea lights. Stir the mixture over low heat and say, "I give this wine to show my love and hope they find it tasty, bring my love into my life and make their arrival hasty." As it cools, thank the goddess of love Freya for her ministrations and then bottle it. Keep it in the fridge until you find the person you feel is worthy of your love.

## Money Comes to Me Potion

**What You Need:**

- 4 cups of water
- 2 sticks of cinnamon
- 4 cloves
- 1 tsp all spice powder
- 2 sprigs of fresh mint
- 2 tsp. brown sugar

Dress your altar in green and gold cloth and light a white candle anointed with your favorite oil. Place three-dollar bills on the altar. Take your cauldron to the kitchen and boil the water and all the other ingredients except the fresh mint for five minutes. Cover the cauldron and let the mixture steep for ten minutes off the heat. Repeat the following "Money and cash are nice to own. They make me happy and fill my soul if the universe wills it to bring that wealth and love to me."

Take the liquid and add the fresh mint. Leave it to cool before straining it and serving it with ice or as a reheated beverage. Feel the emotion you will experience as you receive your rewards while you sip the potion. After you have finished, thank the spirits for their help. For further strength, sprinkle the potion on the dollar bills and leave them on your altar.

## Hocus Focus Potion

**What You Need:**

- 6 fresh lemons
- 4 cups of water
- A sprig of fresh rosemary
- Brown sugar
- Honey
- Lime juice
- Bay leaves
- Glass
- Ice

Make the basic juice by squeezing the lemons into three cups of water. As you squeeze, empower them by visualizing a smarter and sharper you after you have taken the potion. Imagine those awesome ideas you'll have and the positivity flowing from your mind. Set the juice aside to infuse with the rest of the ingredients.

On the stove, heat the remaining water with the rosemary, sugar, and honey. Let it boil for ten minutes until all the sugar has dissolved. Now let the mixture cool as you imagine the success you'll find in the future. That new job or the prospect of new experiences, let your senses become laser-focused on your future.

Add ice to a glass and pour in the lemon liquid. Remove the rosemary sprig and use the sweet liquid to enchant the lemony taste. Create a sweet elixir to promote your mental health and enjoy.

## Bring the Heat Potion

**What You Need:**

- Sprig of rosemary
- ½ tsp thyme
- A pinch of sage
- A pinch of nutmeg
- 2 tsp mint tea leaves
- 3 cloves
- 3 rose petals
- 6 drops of lemon juice
- Water
- Picture of your loved one
- A piece of rose quartz

Set up your altar with red and pink cloths and light three white candles. Set the picture and the quartz in front of the middle white candles. Add the other ingredients to your cauldron and heat them over the candles, or take them into the kitchen and warm them on the stove.

As the mixture cools, repeat the following "Love and heat, fill me with hope and love. Let this tea bring the passion back to my love and me." Strain the liquid and sip it while you visualize the heat you two will bring to the bedroom.

# Conclusion

Congratulations, you have traversed the frozen north and made it to the other side. So, are you now ready to live the life of the Nordic people? Is it the magic that appeals to you or the way of life? It is a personal choice, and however deep you become embroiled in Nordic ways, it's all good! Living a more virtuous life and getting back to basics can make you a better person; throw in some magical knowledge, and you are flying! Magic shouldn't just be something you wonder about, and it should be part of your regular life.

We would all benefit from some enchantment, mystery, and a touch of Nordic happiness, and trolldom is the perfect way to start. Give hygge living and the Scandi ways a try, and you are guaranteed to feel enlightened. Good luck on your journey, and remember to keep Nordic and embrace the trolls.

# Here's another book by Mari Silva that you might like

# Your Free Gift
# (only available for a limited time)

Thanks for getting this book! If you want to learn more about various spirituality topics, then join Mari Silva's community and get a free guided meditation MP3 for awakening your third eye. This guided meditation mp3 is designed to open and strengthen ones third eye so you can experience a higher state of consciousness. Simply visit the link below the image to get started.

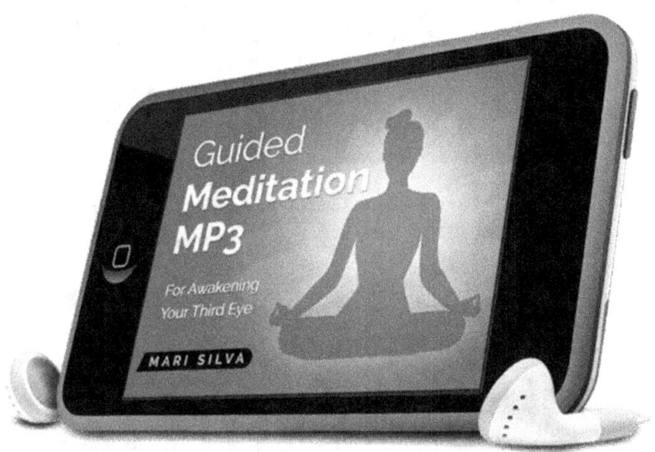


**https://spiritualityspot.com/meditation**

# References

Damian, Angel. "TROLLS! Discover 7 Strange Facts about These Mythical Creatures." Themagichoroscope.com, 29 Jan. 2020, https://themagichoroscope.com/zodiac/mythical-creatures-trolls

"Get to Know the Magic of the Celtic Tree Calendar." Learn Religions, www.learnreligions.com/celtic-tree-months-2562403

"Home." The Trolldom Society, www.thetrolldomsociety.org/.

https://www.facebook.com/bohdi.sanders . "Bodhi Sanders." The Wisdom Warrior, 31 Mar. 2018, https://thewisdomwarrior.com/2010/09/17/the-nine-noble-virtues-viking-values-for-the-warrior-lifestyle/

"My 10 Best Witchcraft Tips for Beginners." Orion the Witch, 7 Aug. 2019, www.orionthewitch.com/10-tips-beginner-witchcraft/#:~:text=My%2010%20Best%20Witchcraft%20Tips%20for%20Beginners%201

"Online Spell Book." Free Witchcraft Spells

Seal, Graham. "THE BLACK BOOK – Dealing with Demons." GRISTLY HISTORY, 1 Dec. 2020, https://gristlyhistory.blog/2020/12/01/the-black-book-dealing-with-demons/

Studios, Clockpunk. "Dwarf Magic." Altearth, www.altearth.net/articles/history-nations/dwarves/dwarf-magic/

team, The Stylist web. "How to Live Nordicly: Achieving Health and Happiness with Tips from the Frozen North." Stylist, 13 June 2016, www.stylist.co.uk/life/how-to-live-nordicly-scandinavia-sweden-norway-denmark-iceland-health-happiness-tips/64781

"The Key of Hell." Astonishing Legends, www.astonishinglegends.com/astonishing-legends/2019/5/11/the-key-of-hell

"The Ultimate Guide to Magical Herbs for Spells & Rituals - TheMagickalCat.com." Www.themagickalcat.com, 18 Nov. 2020, www.themagickalcat.com/magical-herbs-guide

"Using Magical Crystals & Gemstones." Learn Religions, www.learnreligions.com/magical-crystals-and-gemstones-2562758#:~:text=%20Magical%20Crystals%20and%20Gemstones%20%201%20Agate..

"What Are Trolls? Exploring the Mystery of Scandinavian Trolls." Scandification, 30 Jan. 2020, https://scandification.com/exploring-the-mystery-of-scandinavian-trolls/

WiseWitch. "Powerful Cord and Knot Magick." Wise Witches and Witchcraft, 3 July 2018, https://witchcraftandwitches.com/witchcraft/powerful-cord-and-knot-magick/

Yong, Ced. "The Epic List of 250 Legendary Swords from Mythology, Folklore, and Fiction." HobbyLark, https://hobbylark.com/fandoms/The-Epic-List-of-250-Legendary-Swords#:~:text=Mistilteinn%3A%20In%20Norse%20mythology%2C%20the%20magical%20sword%20of

www.ingramcontent.com/pod-product-compliance
Lightning Source LLC
Chambersburg PA
CBHW060622310726
48982CB00003B/639

* 9 7 8 1 6 3 8 1 8 1 9 9 6 *